THE WRITE WAY TO DIE

a Murder By the Book mystery

BETH PRENTICE

THE WRITE WAY TO DIE
Copyright © 2025 by Beth Prentice
Cover design by Daniela Colleo
of www.StunningBookCovers.com

Published by Gemma Halliday Publishing Inc
All Rights Reserved. Except for use in any review, the reproduction or utilization of this work in whole or in part in any form by any electronic, mechanical, or other means, now known or hereafter invented, including xerography, photocopying and recording, or in any information storage and retrieval system is forbidden without the written permission of the publisher, Gemma Halliday.

This is a work of fiction. Names, characters, places, and incidents are either the product of the author's imagination or are used fictitiously, and any resemblance to actual persons, living or dead, business establishments, or events or locales is entirely coincidental.

For Darren—
Because of you, I believe in signs, in whispers from the other side, and in the magic that love leaves behind. You're the reason Aubrey listens for more than just what she can see.

BOOKS BY BETH PRENTICE

Aloha Lagoon Mysteries:
Deadly Wipeout
Lethal Tide
Fatal Break
Tidal Wave

Murder By the Book Mysteries
The Write Way to Die

Saltwater Bay Secrets Mystery Novellas
Murder For Shore

In the recess of the writer's imagination exists a world full of vivid characters with real emotions, their stories just waiting to be told. Some stories are woven with threads of love, others tangled with a web of hate, while a few explore emotions that the writer can barely comprehend. Yet somehow, she conjures a narrative, the words flowing from an unknown well, her story shrouded in the enigma of murder.

…if only I'd known just how easily the line between fiction and fact could blur…

~ Aubrey Jackson

CHAPTER ONE

My first day back in Saltwater Bay wasn't at all what I'd imagined it to be. I mean, it's not like I'd never visited the Virgin Islands before. Nope, I'd visited Grandma Bernie many times over the years, so I knew what to expect on this small island just east of St. Thomas. The temperature was always above bearable, tourists always flooded the shops, and the humidity always doubled the size of my normally sleek dark hair.

But this time was different. I'd never visited without Bernie waiting for me. Yet here I was, three weeks after saying my final goodbye to my beloved grandmother, standing in front of her gorgeous little beach shack, my flip-flops sinking into the soft white sand.

Dropping my suitcase at the bottom of six steps that led to the front porch, I wiped my palms on my denim shorts and squinted against the hot sun as I wrestled with my emotions. On the one hand, the house felt lost and lonely without Bernie bounding out the yellow front door, greeting me with a large smile, and the knowledge that she would never do that again cracked my heart. Yet a flip of excitement that she had left this to me in her will bubbled to the surface.

"Morning Daphne." A deep male voice caused me to jump. I turned to look who was behind me.

"Oh, geez, Grayson, you gave me a fright. Where did you come from?" I gulped.

Grayson Holt had purchased the property next door to Bernie three years ago. At twenty-nine, he was a couple of years older than I was, a good foot taller than I was, had short dark hair and eyelashes most girls envied. He also had a few quirks, but then, who didn't?

This morning, his usually vibrant blue eyes were clouded with concern.

"It's the sand," he explained. "It muffled my footsteps, which is why you didn't hear me approach. But to answer your question, I was around the back of your house. I'm not sure if you knew we had a severe storm last night. With Bernie gone, I've been keeping an eye on the place and wanted to check for any damage."

I smiled. "Well, it's good to see you," I cooed, wanting to give him a hug yet knowing that would make him uncomfortable. Grayson and I were friends, chatting on the phone daily or sending each other funny memes that we'd found on social media. Admittedly, I sent more of those than he did, but he would often surprise me with something silly and hilarious. However, he wasn't a fan of physical contact. Which I'd learned the hard way when I'd given him a hug two Christmases ago and he'd frozen like I'd slapped him. I'd never tried to even shake his hand since then. "It's a bit of a mess around here," I continued, scanning the normally pristine beach.

"The storm coincided with a high tide. The water came up to the path." He nodded toward the cement walkway that meandered its way through palm trees, leading owners and guests from the parking lot to the houses. All the homes were built on wooden poles that kept them safe above the tide line, and it was rare for the water to come this high.

"I guess that explains the shell-covered palm fronds under the porch." I grinned, trying to dispel any unease Grayson may have.

He hated disorder, and I knew the storm debris was probably driving him crazy. But the way he shifted from foot to foot, rubbing the back of his neck, made me feel like this wasn't just about a pile of fronds. And now that I looked closer, he was particularly pale, and his breathing was fast and erratic.

"Grayson, is everything okay?"

"No." His voice was tight. "It's far from okay. Maybe this will be easier to show you. But Daphne"—he hesitated, meeting my gaze—"I warn you, it's not pretty."

Oh geez. That sounded ominous.

"Can I put my suitcase inside first?"

He stared at me for a beat, then picked my case up and took the stairs two at a time. Dropping it at the front door, he then bounded back down. "You need to come see this right away."

Like I said, Grayson had a few quirks, but even this was strange behavior for him.

His steps were at double speed as he turned and moved along the side of the house between his and mine. I hurried to keep up to him, picking my way through broken branches of seagrape tangled with broken shells and coral fragments. Driftwood was draped in seaweed that sat alongside dead jellyfish, and an old pair of sunglasses lay amongst the mess. Urgh! I'd only just arrived and already I had a few days of cleaning up to do.

Grayson rounded the corner ahead of me, his long stride urgent. His shoulders were tense, and his gaze fixed to the ground, leaving me wondering what the hurry was. Only as I caught up with him, he stopped and turned, his pulse visible on his neck as his focus flicked rapidly from me to the sand. I stepped closer, and my breath caught in my throat as my heart rate spiked.

Looking out from beneath the mess was a skull. And judging by the gold tooth that was glinting in the morning sunlight, I was pretty sure it was human.

My chest tightened as I dropped my forehead onto the table and slowly banged it against the wood surface.

"What's wrong?" My BFF Ellie Symonds reached across and rubbed my back, her concern evident in her tone. My head shot up to see a lock of her copper curls fall over her eye, and she absently brushed it away. At five-foot-two Ellie was a bundle of sunshine, her smile fast and contagious. Until you rubbed her up the wrong way. Then her temper was as fiery as her hair.

"I can't do this," I whined, anxiously tugging at the neckline of my pink sweater, my temperature rising with every breath. "I've rewritten this scene about twenty times now, and it's still not gripping enough. I've lost it, Ellie. I've lost my ability to write!"

"Aubrey, take a deep breath. I can see the panic lurking in those big brown eyes of yours. I'm sure you're exaggerating."

"No, I'm not. Read it. See for yourself." I slammed back against my cream fur-lined jacket hanging over the hard chair, and ran my palm across my scalp, and my fingers knotted in my messy bun.

Ellie pushed up the sleeves of her multi-colored knitted sweater and squinted as her hazel eyes danced over my words. "Oh, I love the title—*Murder for Shore*." Her smile was bright, but only momentarily. Quickly her lips pressed together, and her shoulders slumped. Once she'd finished, her wide grin became forced. "The tropics?"

"Yeah, we may not have snow yet, but I'm sick of the cold already." I shrugged, enjoying that my imaginary world was warm. "But what do you think of the writing?"

"It's fine," she said, once again rubbing my back.

"Fine? Fine is not good enough." I winced as my ring caught on a long blond lock.

"Aubrey, it's the first chapter. Give yourself a break." Her nose crinkled, and her freckles clumped together, making her look younger than her twenty-eight years.

I sighed. It was alright for her. She had three hit novels to her name. I'd yet to write one.

"Yes, but the first chapter has to be the most compelling part of the book. You know that. Willow just spoke for a whole hour on the subject." I huffed and unhooked my hair as I pointed toward the woman silhouetted against a presentation board as she sat signing paperback copies of her latest *New York Times* best-selling novel.

Willow Fox wasn't her real name, but she suited it. Her graceful limbs elegantly glided through the air as she flicked her long inky black tresses over her shoulder. Her full lips turned into a smile and her perfectly plucked eyebrows arched over her sharp emerald green eyes that never missed a detail. She was beautiful, commanded attention, and was the envy of everyone in the room.

She'd recently co-written a novel with Jenna Mulgrady, a mutual friend of ours. When it had become a number one bestseller, we'd all cheered for Jenna. And when Willow announced she was running her first writers' retreat in *my* hometown, where she would share her knowledge and wisdom of how to become that successful, I jumped at the chance to learn. Even if the admission price of two thousand dollars was a lot higher than I was comfortable with. But then Jenna had explained to me that it covered the cost of accommodation, meals, and classes. And depending on how well it went or didn't, Willow may never run a second retreat, so how could I miss an opportunity like that?

Before today, I'd never been to a writing retreat, but Ellie and Jenna had both convinced me it was a great idea. To be honest, I was totally nervous about the entire weekend, not really knowing what to expect. But the itinerary was pretty simple. Lots of time to sit quietly and write. One group session today where Willow spoke about honing our craft, another group session tomorrow filled with advice on how to get an agent, which hopefully would lead to getting a publishing deal with one of the big-name publishers, and one session on marketing and branding, followed by a one-on-one manuscript assessment. That was the draw card. To have Willow read my work was a dream come true, and I knew a lot of writers would kill for the chance that I'd been given. Thank goodness for friends in high places, right? Without Jenna, I never would have been one of the six chosen attendees. Now I sat alongside Ellie, not quite believing I was here.

I took a deep breath and inhaled the history of the room surrounding me. Once an elegant reception area, the leather studded lounges had been temporarily pushed back to the walls to allow for the tables and chairs to be placed in three rows. The wood parquet flooring had been covered with a heavily patterned blue rug, the walls were oak paneled, and the two floor-to-ceiling windows flanked Willow. The four other participants had their heads down, fingers flying over the keyboard of their laptops, lost in the worlds they were creating. Willow's enthusiasm was inspiring—it just wasn't a miracle when it came to my work.

"She's like the horse whisperer for authors," I murmured.

"She is pretty incredible."

"How does she look that good when she spends eight hours a day sitting at a computer writing? I know my butt's already spreading, and most days, I can barely be bothered to brush my hair. And don't even get me started on makeup." I'd slunk low in my chair when Willow had recommended we treat our writing as a day job by getting ready as if meeting our boss.

Ellie laughed. "Oh please. You don't need makeup. You're effortlessly beautiful."

"And that's why I love you, my friend." Despite Ellie living close to forty miles away in Snohomish, we managed to catch up with each other at least once a month. Phone calls were daily, but to spend an entire weekend with her was rare.

"It happens to be true. If I didn't love you back, I'd hate you. No one should be able to eat like you do and still be that petite without going to the gym. Plus, I'd kill for lashes like yours." Ellie gave me a fake scowl, the crinkle around her eyes betraying her humor.

"Hmmm, that might be a good motive for murder." I scribbled on the pad next to my laptop. "Victim killed for having great lashes."

Ellie laughed, and one of our retreat friends glared over her shoulder.

"Can you girls keep it down?" she warned, pushing her gray hair back from her face.

"What's wrong, Nancy?" Ellie asked. "You look troubled."

"Troubled? Well, I guess that's a word for it."

"Are your characters not playing nice today?"

"My characters are just fine! It's this stupid laptop I'm struggling with." At seventy-four, Nancy was writing her debut novel, and it wasn't the first time that technology had tripped her up. But who could blame her? I was twenty-eight and had grown up using a computer, and more often than not, technology tripped me up too.

"Anything I can do to help?"

"Only if you know why I have all these extra symbols on my screen. They weren't there ten minutes ago, and I have no idea how to get rid of them." She gave an exasperated sigh and sat straight as she yanked at the hem of her black cable-knit sweater, her fingers fidgeting with the wool.

I looked over her shoulder and noted all the red writing and words underlined with squiggly lines.

"You have your Track Changes on," I commented, feeling pretty pleased with myself that I knew the answer to that one.

"What are they?" Behind her oversized glasses, Nancy squinted her light brown eyes, her lips pursed, a well dug vertical crease evident between her brows.

"It's how you track what changes you made to the document," Ellie explained. "Just turn them off."

"I have no idea how I turned them on in the first place!" Nancy flopped back in her chair, defeat oozing from every pore.

"Let me show you." Ellie pushed her chair backwards and moved to squat alongside Nancy. A few taps of the keys later, and Nancy breathed a sigh of relief.

"Oh, thank goodness. I was worried it would look like that forever."

"That was an easy one." Ellie beamed. As the more tech savvy of the two of us, most things seemed easy to Ellie.

Willow glanced in our direction. "Is everything okay, ladies?"

Ellie nodded vigorously. Nancy was already engrossed in her words again, her brow low, two-finger typing at a painfully slow rate.

Willow smiled knowingly before she turned her attention away from us as her sister, Isla, entered the make-shift conference room. Closing the cover of the book she was signing, Willow stood and made her way toward Isla, her loose-fitting pants swirling around her legs as black patent Louboutins clicked on the floorboards.

The two sisters held their heads close together as Isla whispered something, and the differences between the women were stark.

Whereas Willow was tall, Isla was on the shorter side. Isla's shoulder-length tawny brown bob contrasted against the Willow's long dark locks. They both had the same commanding presence and the same sharp green eyes, and Isla held herself with the same grace, yet there was something more human and approachable about her. Despite the scowl she presently wore.

My thoughts flashed to my own sister, Emily, and pain stabbed at my heart. Before her accident, we'd been close, often finishing each other's sentences, fighting over the same pair of jeans, and swooning over Ryan Reynolds. But that all changed the night she fell asleep behind the wheel while driving and never came home.

"She's struggling to have children," Ellie whispered, leaning in close.

I flinched as my thoughts shot back to the present. "What?"

"It's why Willow purchased this place."

I raised an eyebrow, not quite connecting the dots.

Ellie took a quick breath. "Remember how you told Jenna that your blogger friend The Roaming Reporter did a story on

Stoney Creek? Well, Jenna told Willow about it, and the article convinced Willow that this was the perfect place to bring Isla for a girls' weekend."

I nodded, keeping up so far.

"While they were here, Isla fell in love with the peace and tranquility of the area," Ellie continued. "So Willow purchased The Grand Hotel because she knew that Isla and her husband Chris were having financial difficulties after four rounds of IVF. She did it to give them a job and to help them find a quiet life where Isla may just find it easier to conceive. How amazing is that?" Ellie gave a blissful sigh.

The Stoney Creek gossip mill had run rampant with the news that the famous Willow Fox had purchased The Grand Hotel and had relocated her sister and brother-in-law from California to run it as a B&B. And whenever one of her celebrity friends visited and were spotted in town, we all feigned nonchalance and then immediately snapped a sneaky selfie and posted it on The Creek's community Facebook page.

"Four rounds? Geez, her hormones would be raging," I commented, glad it wasn't me. Not that I had anything against children, but I just wasn't at that stage of life yet. Nor did I have a man, and as he was an important part in getting pregnant, I figured my time might be a way off yet.

Ellie bit her lip and absently rubbed her stomach.

"Wait a minute! Is there something you're not telling me?" Butterflies zipped in my belly as I eagerly awaited her reply, and any anxiety I had felt about my career vanished. "Are you and Joel trying for a baby?" Ellie had married her other best friend last year in a glorious ceremony of sunshine, flowers, and joy. A baby would complete her.

"No." She dropped her hand and slumped backwards, her smile momentarily disappearing.

"Ellie..."

She gave a heavy sigh. "Okay, we're trying."

I squealed, and Nancy looked over her shoulder and hit me with a glare.

"Sorry," I mouthed to her before turning to Ellie.

"This is why I didn't tell you," Ellie whispered. "You always get overexcited."

"But it's fantastic news!"

"It would be if everything was happening the way it was supposed to."

"I've heard it takes time."

"But what if it doesn't? What if it never happens? What if I'm like Isla?"

"Don't get ahead of yourself. Relax and let nature do what it does best."

"With advice like that, you should be writing a romance instead of a mystery."

Hmmm, she might have a point there. Maybe I could turn the steam up on my mystery.

I picked up my pen and bit the end of it as I frowned at my screen. The low-level anxiety that constantly sat heavily on my shoulders twinged. I hadn't mentioned it to anyone as it was something that I hated to admit even to myself, but if I didn't write a bestseller, I was going to have to consider taking the bakery job my mom kept offering me. Don't get me wrong. Working in Mom's bakery definitely had its perks, but writing was what I loved. Stories and the possibilities they held excited my soul, and I adored getting lost in new realms that I'd created.

It was something I'd done as a child. When life got hard, I would curl up on my bed, close my eyes, and imagine a world that was filled with love and laughter and magic. One where I controlled everything. As I'd grown, I'd learned to write those stories down, but it had taken me a very long time to allow anyone to read my words. They were so personal to me that I'd felt physical pain when anyone criticized them. Of course, my English teacher had said that criticism was a good thing as it was how I learned to make those stories better, to show the reader how to enter my worlds rather than tell them. I'd worked tirelessly on my craft and relished every second I'd spent perfecting my tales, but selling them was a whole other entity.

Rubbing the heel of my palm against my brow, I jumped as Spencer Stratford leaned across the table behind me.

"You're spending more time procrastinating than you are typing. Writer's block hitting hard again?"

Spencer and I had been friends for the last six months, but every time I looked at him, a barrage of butterflies erupted in my stomach.

"Yes." I swiveled on my chair to face him and instantly got lost in the blue depths of his eyes and the musky scent of his aftershave. Momentarily, I was lost for words.

Oh boy.

"How's your latest novel panning out?" Ellie asked him, as it seemed I'd lost use of my voice.

"I've just killed off a character that I hated." His dazzling smile flashed and sucked the last of the oxygen from my lungs. At six feet four, Spencer towered over most people. His rugged jawline, raw sensuality, and boyish charm caused very inappropriate tingles, but what made me so attracted to him was his quick wit and caring nature.

"Did you give him a slow, painful death?"

"The worst!" His eyes twinkled.

"Is this character based on a real-life person?" I croaked, attempting to gain some control of my emotions.

"Maybe." He shrugged, yet his mischievous grin betrayed him.

"Spencer, how is it that you can't even kill a bug in real life, yet the thrillers you write are dark and disturbing?"

"I prefer my murders to be fictional. Less mess." He winked, and I nearly fell off my chair.

"You have one seriously twisted mind," Ellie added with a giggle. "Come on, tell us who the victim really is?"

He glanced left to right before closing his laptop and signaling to us that we move closer. "Do you know the guy that runs this place?"

I nodded and lowered my elbow onto the table between us. "Yeah. Willow's brother-in-law, Chris Woods."

Spencer's grin widened. "Well, this morning, he was super rude to me, so I decided to get my revenge."

"What did he do?" I needed to know how to stay off Spencer's victim list.

"I was in the dining room when he came storming in, yelling at someone on his cell phone about how 'they're not going to get away with this'." Spencer's long fingers lifted in air quotes. "I happened to be standing in the walkway, and instead of sidestepping me, he almost shoulder charged me out of the way. I made my decision then and there that it was time for him to go." He chuckled, obviously happy with himself.

"That's a harsh punishment," I mused.

"Yeah well, he seems like a jerk to me. Now he's the star corpse of my latest novel. Fitting punishment I believe."

"Keep your voice down," cautioned Ellie in a whisper. "His wife Isla's standing behind you."

I glanced over Spencer's shoulder as he shrugged, noting Willow and Isla still deep in conversation. Isla impatiently tapped her watch, and Willow nodded as she turned to face the room.

"Okay all!" She clapped her hands to get everyone's attention. "I can see that you're working hard, getting those words on the page, but we need a break. Sustenance is very important for the creative spirit. I know I can't think straight unless I've had at least one cupcake and a cup of coffee." Her tinkling laugh was met by agreeing murmurs as fingers froze on keyboards and our group looked up and blinked.

The sound of laptops closing and chairs scraping was quickly drowned out as my fellow writers slowly left their imaginary worlds behind and started to chat.

I looked at the words I'd written and sighed.

Maybe Willow was right, and I just needed a cupcake.

* * *

Stoney Creek sat to the north of Serenity Lake and was a quiet little town nestled amongst the hills and dense forest of the Pacific Northwest. Our population was just over ten thousand. Most of the houses were a mix of old-world charm and modern coziness, with many of them boasting wraparound porches and high rooflines. In the summer, hanging baskets filled with cheerful flowers adorned those porches, and residents could often be found enjoying a beer in their rocking chairs and waving to the neighborhood as it passed by. Downtown shops were locally owned, the architecture dated back to the late 1800s, and the air was crisp and clean. In winter however, residents retreated inside for warmth. The flowers faded, and the creek would often freeze. Overlooking the breathtaking view of the lake, The Grand Hotel sat high on the hill on the edge of Stoney Creek. It was two stories of Victorian stone work, a wraparound porch, and a real turret complete with room at the top.

As a result of being an adult and not having enough money to purchase a real house, I now lived in a tiny houseboat moored within a small community at the edge of Serenity Lake. It wasn't one of those fancy houseboats that you see in the movies. Nope, mine was the kind you see sold "as is" and was constantly in need of one repair or another. It had ugly brown siding and was barely big enough to swing a cat. My mom hated it and always worried about me, especially in the winter. But once I'd overcome the constant movement as the gentle waves lapped at the sides, I'd grown to love it. And the advantage was that from my living-room window I had the perfect view of the cliffs and the hotel. A view I couldn't afford otherwise.

As a child, I'd always been fascinated by the hotel, and whenever we drove past, I'd imagined a beautiful princess living within the walls, the acres of gardens filled with wildlife. The truth was the beautiful princess had been a middle-aged widow who lived her life pushing the boundaries of convention. She had died prematurely, willing the property to her best friend to use in any way she saw fit as long as it benefited wildlife rescue. Apparently, Willow offered an obscene amount of money for it, which made the wildlife rescue society very happy indeed. Win-win for everyone involved, I guess.

I'd lived in Stoney Creek my entire life, only leaving to study creative writing at Seattle University. I'd met Jenna and Ellie in a study group there, and we'd quickly become best friends, instantly bonding over a storyline and spending our summer writing what was going to be our breakthrough bestseller. The reality was that we ended up with an average book but a friendship that had withstood the highs and lows of life. Despite not reaching the career highs that Jenna had, I was happy to say we were still close.

"Geez, that's some spread." Spencer rubbed his hands together as he eyed the buffet laid out on a long table opposite the dark wood bar. The room looked like it pulled double duties, with a couch and comfortable chairs at one end and a bar with stools at the other, where our retreat friend, Kara, was already ordering a drink.

As an author of erotic fiction, Kara oozed sexuality, and today she looked glorious in her thigh-high boots, skinny jeans, and a tight red waist coat which complemented her confidence. When I'd first been introduced to her, I'd been slightly intimidated, and once she'd offered to act out any BDSM that I may need to research, I had politely declined and kept my distance. I blushed even thinking of it.

"If you ladies will excuse me, I'm getting a piece of that mud cake before it disappears."

Ellie laughed. "He has a metabolism like yours. He can eat whatever he wants and still has the body of a god."

I glanced down at the waistline of my jeans and grimaced. Best not to bring her attention to that.

Thankfully, one of our retreat friends moved in close beside me.

"Aren't those curtains divine, Aubrey?" Beverley smiled reverently.

I followed her eyeline and noted how the velvet curtains, wainscoting, and marble mantel surrounding a roaring fire all made the room feel much cozier than it should.

"Ummm..." To be honest, the curtains would have looked great in my Gran's house, but they weren't really to my taste. But then Beverley was closer to my Gran's age than she was to mine, so maybe it was a generation thing.

She pushed her hot pink rimmed glasses up the bridge of her wide nose, her appreciation of the room evident in her genuine smile. With her large bosom, knitted kaftan, and yellow beret perched jauntily on her black curls, she made everyone around her look beige.

"Umm, sure," I replied to Beverley, referring to the curtains.

"They suit this room to perfection."

I smiled, not really sure how to respond to that. "Did you get a lot of writing done in that last session?" I asked instead.

"Yes! There's something special about this building that's bringing out the best in me. Something very romantic about it."

She was right. If you were into old school romance, then this place could certainly enhance the mood.

"How did you do?" she asked me.

"Well, I write mystery, so the ambience hasn't really helped." Even though, looking toward Spencer as he licked the cream off the chocolate cake, I wondered if maybe I'd underestimated the place.

Beverley laughed. "Well, let's hope it presents you with a nice mystery to unravel and help with your writing."

"Wouldn't that be exciting!" Ellie bounced on her toes, her fingers clasped together and a gleam in her eye.

"My mom always told me to be careful what you wish for." I shivered as a chill danced down my spine. A chill I didn't believe had anything to do with the fact I'd forgotten my jacket.

"That's very true. I guess we should all be happy to have the time to learn and get those words on the page, uninterrupted by the real world. Isn't that what retreats are really for?" Ellie shrugged.

"Maybe the next one we go to can be somewhere warm?" I inquired. "It's freezing today."

"My knee tells me that it will be snowing by Monday," Beverley explained, showing her stockinged leg from under her long dress. "And it never gets it wrong."

"Snow will be nice," Ellie mused.

"When I'm home and don't have to go out for a week maybe," I added, screwing up my nose.

"How can you not like the snow?" Ellie asked. "You miss all the fun of building snowmen and snowball fights."

"I'm good with missing those, thanks. But I am partial to a hot cocoa and snuggling in front of a roaring fire." I grinned.

Beverley's smile faded as she glanced toward the buffet table, and her gaze landed on Spencer. "It's been lovely chatting with you ladies, but Nancy's asked me to save her a piece of cake. I'd better act quick before Spencer eats it all."

She may just be too late as he was already demolishing a second piece of chocolate cake and was helping himself to a caramel slice. Fast metabolism or not, he'd better slow down or those jeans may just hug that athletic backside a little tighter.

As Beverley pushed her way through the small group, our friend Jenna stepped across the deep red carpet toward us, her rosebud lips pursed as strain showed on her round face.

"What's he doing here?" she muttered, stopping next to me, her gaze falling on the man who had just moved in alongside Spencer. The man wasn't bad looking if you were into awkward thirty somethings with a boyish charm. His dark disheveled hair touched the collar of his leather jacket which he'd left open, displaying his V-neck T-shirt that could no longer contain the copious amounts of chest hair. Geez, had he never heard of clippers?

"Gate crasher?" I asked, putting my arm around my friend's shoulder and giving her a squeeze. Despite her being one of the event coordinators, I'd barely seen her since we'd arrived this morning.

"Maybe he stopped by for a coffee," Ellie added, her smile large and fast.

"Or something stronger," I added. "He looks pretty drunk to me." The man swayed as he lifted a glass of amber liquid to his lips.

"This is a private function. Security was supposed to only allow guests to be in here."

"He's not hurting anyone, and it looks like he's got Spencer enthralled in conversation, which means we may have a chance at getting a cinnamon roll before he eats them all." Ellie laughed.

Jenna smoothed an imaginary stray auburn curl as she straightened her already pristine shirt. "Willow will have a fit if she sees him."

"Why? Who is he?"

"Ricky Campbell. And I honestly have no idea what's going on, but Willow's personal assistant told me that Willow didn't want him here, and if I saw him, then I was to have him removed. ASAP."

Ellie shrugged. "Willow needs to calm down. Now are you both coming to get something to eat?"

"Grab me a cupcake, will you, please?" I asked, eyeing a sprinkle-topped delight.

"Sure." Ellie beamed as she moved past the small group of romance writers, all with their heads together, their hands doing most of the talking.

I sighed as I turned to Jenna, noting the dark rings shining beneath her makeup. "You look tired."

"I didn't sleep well last night. Willow made a few last-minute changes to the presentation, and it was up to me to update the PowerPoint slides."

"Why didn't she do it? She's a part of this, just like you are."

"She was busy putting the finishing touches to her latest manuscript."

"And it couldn't have waited?"

"Apparently not." Jenna gave me a sideways glance. "Don't look at me like that. I talked Willow into doing this retreat, so it's my job to make sure it runs smoothly."

"Why did you do that?"

"Because it's good money. I mean it wouldn't be if Willow didn't own this place, but once I have all the teething issues sorted, then four thousand dollars per participant is easy money."

"I only paid half that."

"Yeah, I gave you and Ellie a discount. But don't tell the others." She beamed as I showed my gratitude with a hug.

"That's a lot of money, but with Willow's success, surely she doesn't need it," I added.

"She told me that it's time to give back. Being able to help new writers get started gave her inspiration." Jenna shrugged. "I didn't really care why she agreed to it. I was just happy that we could give it a shot because she may not need the cash, but I do."

"Ellie and Spencer are hardly new writers."

"They're an exception." She wiggled her eyebrows, and I giggled. It paid to have friends in the right places.

"Oh geez." Jenna's smile gave way to the stress once again pulling at her lips. "Here comes Naomi. I'd better get Ricky out of here before she sees him."

Jenna scurried across the room, leaving me to wonder if all this work was really going to pay off.

"Sometimes I envy her, but other times, I'm not so sure," Ellie commented, moving back in alongside me and handing me a cupcake. "Success comes at a price."

"True. I wouldn't mind the use of Willow's assistant though. There are times when she'd come in very handy." I nodded toward Naomi who was presently standing with her hands on her hips, death staring Ricky as Jenna hurried him from the room.

Ellie giggled. "I know what you mean. Not sure if I'd choose Naomi though. She comes across as a bit …"

"Bossy," I finished.

"I was going to say scary, but I like your description better."

"Oh geez, she's heading our way. I'm going to the bathroom before she can ask me once again to write a review for Willow's retreat."

"Is she annoying you with that too?" Ellie's brow crinkled.

"Uh-huh. Oops, sorry I've got to go." I hurriedly wrapped the cupcake in a napkin and dropped it into my tote bag.

"Me too!"

"It'll look obvious if we both suddenly need the bathroom," I hissed, grabbing Ellie's arm.

"Then what do you suggest I do?" Ellie's eyes were wide as she scoured the room.

"Go and chat with Spencer. He looks lonely without Ricky."

"Good idea." As I watched Ellie close in on Spencer, the little green monster sitting on my shoulder whispered I should have swapped places with her. But the thought of being alone with him made the idea of hiding out in the lady's bathroom much more appealing.

My growing feelings for Spencer were going to have to be addressed at some point, but today, I had more pressing issues on my mind, and I needed to focus on my career. Real-life romance could wait, right?

Keeping my head down to avoid eye contact with Naomi, I made my way from the room, exhaling contentedly as I stepped into the cool hallway. The chatter and sounds of clinking cups and glasses drifted into background noise as I made my way past the dark oak staircase toward my destination.

"Aubrey. Is everything okay?"

I looked up into the strained face of Isla, noting how her smile didn't make it all the way to her watery eyes.

"Yes, just looking for the little girls' room."

Isla nodded. "Second door on the left."

"Thank you. Oh, and I wanted to say how excited I am for the weekend ahead. I can't wait for my one-on-one session with Willow!"

"Great. Willow will be pleased." A dark vein near her temple throbbed. "I hope you're finding the hotel to your liking. If not, please let Chris know as he's in charge of the event location, and he can attend to anything you need." She swallowed hard, her jaw tense.

"That's so kind of you, but honestly everything is perfect."

"Fantastic. Well, I hope you find the rest of the weekend beneficial, and you learn a lot. Now if you'll excuse me, there's something I need to attend to."

"Work never stops," I trilled.

"Apparently." With that, she clicked away, her heels carrying her at double speed.

I took my time in the bathroom, enjoying the silence as I regathered my thoughts. Spencer had already sent me a text message asking where I was, Ellie had tagged me in two memes on Instagram, and my mom had sent me three messenger messages asking about dinner next week. As I was trying to focus on my storyline, I ignored them all, finished what I needed to do, touched up my mascara, dabbed some clear lip gloss on my rosebud lips, and then made my way back toward the group, knowing that our break would nearly be over. I had a career to focus on, and I didn't want to miss any of the wisdom Willow was ready to pass along.

I must have channeled her as her voice filled the air, causing me to stop in my tracks.

"You're not allowed to be here, Levi!" she yelled.

Wowzers, that sounded intense. I looked into the room marked *Manager* and saw her take a large step backwards. She stopped with her hands by her side, her fists clenching and unclenching as her eyes fired daggers at a man standing opposite her. His slumped shoulders, broody pout, lean body, and tousled dark hair gave him a vulnerability that quickly stole my heart as he lovingly stared back at her.

"But-but I'm not here to hurt you. I only wanted to wish you well on the sale of your latest novel." He gently offered his hand toward her as he took a step closer. "It's a big deal getting an offer from Heron and Heron Publishing."

"How... how do you know about that?" she spat, her eyebrows getting lost in her bangs. "No one knows about that yet." Her voice lowered as she quickly scanned the room.

Heron and Heron? Wow, that *was* a big deal. I slunk back into the shadows outside the door, unable to move away but not wanting to be caught eavesdropping. Luckily, a silver framed mirror on the far wall of the room reflected the drama back to me.

"It doesn't matter how I know," the man replied. "I'm happy for you. You deserve it." His smile was large and genuine, yet Willow tensed.

"Oh my goodness, have you been going through my personal files again? You do remember I have a restraining order preventing you from being anywhere near me?"

"No, I haven't been anywhere near your personal files. That's silly. And you know that I'd never hurt you, babe."

"Don't call me that! You lost that privilege when you were sleeping with my assistant."

He visibly tensed. His breath was loud and controlled as his eyes narrowed, and his voice came hard and fast. "That was a lie. I've never as much as kissed Naomi. I would never do anything to hurt you, and you know it."

"I know nothing of the sort. Now get out of here before I call the police." She had a white knuckled grip on her cell phone as she waved it toward him.

He sized her up as his jaw flexed, and my heart jumped into my throat. Suddenly, he didn't look so vulnerable. "You need to be reasonable. Think clearly," he said, moving to stand over her.

Willow licked her lips before straightening her back and squaring up to him. "I had complete clarity the day I kicked you out of my life. Now be a good boy and get away from me. Or I promise you will live to regret it."

His eyes closed, his body stiffened, and my breath caught. Just as I thought I'd pass out from lack of oxygen, Levi relaxed his shoulders and took a large step backwards.

"Fine. We'll talk another day." He lifted his hands in surrender.

"No. We most certainly won't." Willow pushed her way past him, her lips tight, her step fast. As she closed the gap between us, I didn't wait to see what happened next. Instead, I scurried from my hiding spot and ducked into an adjoining closet. If Willow knew I'd overheard something so personal, I wouldn't need to worry about writer's block. My career would be dead in the water.

My knees felt shaky as I peered through a crack around the door and watched her march toward the stairs. Once she was out of my sight, I released the breath I'd been holding and hurried back to the function room, the sound of happy chatter soothing me as the aroma of coffee called my name.

"You okay?" Spencer asked, his dark brow knotted as he considered me.

"Yeah. Of course. Why wouldn't I be?" I stepped past him and poured myself a large cup of coffee. The pot rattled against the cup I was holding as the black liquid slopped over the sides and onto the plush carpet. Darn it.

"You don't look it." Spencer reached across and took both the cup and the pot from me, successfully pouring my drink. Leading me to a nearby chair, he held out his hand offering me to sit. I flopped onto the sumptuous cushion and accepted the cup of liquid heaven. My soul released a deep contented sigh.

"Now, what's shaken you?"

Inhaling the scent of the coffee, I took a calming breath. "I just overheard something I shouldn't have."

"Care to share?"

Glancing around to ensure no one else was within earshot, I lowered my voice and leaned in close to Spencer. That was mistake number one as he smelled all kinds of good. His breath tickled my cheek, and I suddenly lost my train of thought. Mistake number two came when I parted my lips to form words, and nothing but a small pleasurable groan escaped.

Spencer's eyebrows pulled together as his gaze darted to my mouth.

Thankfully, Ellie appeared and saved me from any more embarrassment as she dropped into a soft leather chair alongside me, putting her head close to mine and Spencer's.

"What am I missing?" she asked.

Heat raced up my neck, flushing my cheeks and causing both my friends to gaze at me with deep V's between their brows. I gulped, about to bring them both up-to-date when Beverley dinged her glass to get our attention.

"Excuse me all, but our session was supposed to start five minutes ago. I know we haven't been called, but maybe we should make our way back."

Murmurs around the room seemed to concur with her, and slowly our group dissipated, making their way toward their laptops.

"Aubrey, are you okay?" Ellie asked.

"Yep. I'll bring you up-to-date later. As it stands, I think we should get back to it."

Willow hadn't been in the best of moods, and the last thing I needed was to upset her even more.

* * *

"What do you think of this?" I sat back and scrubbed my face with my hands as what I hoped were irrational worries about my manuscript ran through my mind causing my stomach to churn. I'd just finished rewriting my opening scene. Again. And now I needed Ellie's opinion.

As she read my words, I briefly questioned my decision to give up the safety of my job at the local post office to chase my dreams. But after losing Emily, I knew I had to be doing something that I loved, so I'd used my accrued annual leave, drained my savings, and given myself six months to complete my first book. The thought of being a published author had caused a ripple of excitement to flood my belly, but I'd quickly learned that, in reality, it was nowhere near as glamorous as Willow made it look. And to replace the steady paycheck I once had, this book had to be an instant hit.

"Let me see," she offered, reading over my shoulder. "Oh, I love it! Tell me, will there be a budding romance happening between Grayson and Daphne?"

I grinned. "Every story needs a little romance, right?"

"Never a truer word has been said. Who's Grayson modeled after?"

"No one," I gushed, ignoring the wicked glint in her eye.

"Whatever." She giggled.

"Where's Willow?" Spencer asked. I jumped. "We were supposed to start the final session of the day thirty minutes ago."

"Last I saw her she went upstairs. Maybe she lost track of time."

"I wouldn't worry," Ellie added. "It gives us some extra time to work on our stories." Her gaze darted back to her notes, her thought process written in the deep crevices of her frown.

Not everyone had joined the afternoon session, some instead choosing to work privately in their rooms, but those here seemed to have had the same idea as all that could be heard was the clicking of keys and the occasional loud breath.

Ellie flicked the pages of her notes as she bit her lip, and Spencer went back to his own work.

Okay, come on Aubrey. You can do this. You're already in love with your new male lead so keep writing. You just need to flesh him out. But what comes next?

Forcing my fingers to move, I closed my eyes and thought of my story. Within seconds, my hero's baby blue eyes filled my mind, and the sound of his voice caused me to sigh wistfully.

"Do you have that reference book I loaned you?" he asked, his deep baritone filling my head.

Huh? That didn't sound right.

"Aubrey. Sorry to interrupt your thoughts, but I was hoping to spend the afternoon rereading it." I opened my eyes to see Spencer staring at me intently. Had it been his voice I'd heard when thinking of my good-looking hero? Oh geez. I was in real trouble.

"Ummm, sure." I attempted to clear my emotions as I rummaged through my oversized tote, searching for the book in question. "Darn it. I think I left it in the car."

"Don't stress. I can get it off you later."

"It's okay. Willow still isn't here, so I'm sure I have a few minutes to duck out and get it." And the cool autumn air would give me a chance to reset.

Spencer nodded. "Only if it's no problem. It's just I wanted to run over some emotional wounds and how they impact a character's decision-making before I got too far into this chapter I'm working on."

Pulling my car keys from the depths of my bag, I dropped my cell phone into the back pocket of my jeans, scraped my chair backwards, and stood. "I won't be long."

I quietly padded past my fellow authors, trying my best not to disturb them, and stepped into the foyer of the hotel, smiling at Chris as he made his way down the grand staircase that wound its way around the walls. I'd only met Chris briefly when I first arrived, but his sense of style, lean frame, steel blue eyes, high cheekbones, and chiseled jawline gave him a movie star quality. Only I could see why Spencer had taken a dislike to him, as he ignored me, his look dark as he stormed toward the rear of the house.

I shrugged and pulled open the door. The fresh air instantly hit me hard, and I shivered against the cold autumn breeze that brought with it the citrusy scent of the Douglas firs. Traffic sounds were distant as the tall trees that surrounded the property kept the world and its chaos at bay. The clear afternoon sky was dotted with a gang of birds flying in their classic V pattern, headed to warmer climates, and snow had started to fall on the distant mountain tops. I loved Stoney Creek and the change of seasons, but I really wished I'd remembered to bring a jacket with me.

Picking up my pace, I rounded the building and was making my way toward the parking lot when a ground squirrel raced across my path. Unlike a lot of people I knew, I loved squirrels. My gaze followed it into the nearby gardens that surrounded the building. It was then I noticed some of the bushes were broken. As everything else was immaculately pruned, ready for the winter ahead, I thought it was odd.

The squirrel squeaked loudly and shot back out of the garden at full speed. Something had scared it, and it made me curious.

Stepping closer to the branches, I sucked in a large fast breath as I recognized the red sole of a pair of Louboutins. Willow Fox was lying on her back, her neck twisted at a very odd angle, her eyes open and unfocused. Dead.

CHAPTER TWO

———

The grounds of the Hotel had been transformed from peaceful gardens of serenity to a hive of activity and noise. The police officers who had initially arrived quickly called for backup, and now the air was filled with the crackle of their radios. Their voices mingled into background noise as they strung crime scene tape around the area, held onlookers at bay, and took statements from all those they could. It was organized chaos, yet I felt distanced and cold, and in the fading afternoon light, I struggled to pull my thoughts together.

At well over six-foot-tall and with more muscles than a front cover of a men's health magazine, Detective Jacob Tate exuded strength and confidence. But as he looked down at me, his smoke gray eyes were wide. One large hand held a well-loved notebook while the other ran through his short blond hair. A tiny bead of sweat formed on the edge of his manscaped stubble as he hurriedly glanced over his extremely broad shoulder. The movement caused his white cotton shirt to ride up ever so slightly, giving me a glimpse of an abdomen that took a workout seriously. My heart rate had definitely picked up, but I was putting that down to stress.

Turning his attention back to me, his brow lowered. "Aubrey, I know this is very distressing for you, but I need answers to some questions, and I can't understand what you're saying." His deep voice held a hint of hysteria. I had no idea why. I was only crying, and surely, a crying woman wasn't that scary for a homicide detective. Especially one the size of him that oozed virile masculinity.

"I'm, I'm s-so... sorry," I hiccupped, snuggling into the warm jacket he'd slipped off and handed to me. One that I could almost wrap around myself twice. "I... I've never... never seen a real d-dead body before."

"I understand. I really do, but I need you to recount how you found the body."

I nodded before loudly blowing my nose into a sopping wet tissue. Detective Tate grimaced and called to a nearby uniformed officer. "Can anyone give us some help here, please?" His finger twirled in my direction.

The female officer gave me a sympathetic look before ducking into a waiting patrol car, its flashing red and blue lights giving her an eerie glow. While we waited, Tate frowned and slid his hands into the pockets of his faded denim jeans all the while giving me sidelong glances before looking like he wanted to run.

"Take some slow deep breaths," the female officer said once she'd returned and handed me a tissue box. "It activates the parasympathetic nervous system. Your body has no choice but to slow both your heart rate and your breathing."

I hugged the new box to my chest and breathed in to the count of three, trying my best to focus. I'll happily report that it worked, and the tightness that gripped my chest eased. Well, that was until I saw the coroner lifting Willow into a body bag.

The loss of life was overwhelming, and my sobbing quickly turned up a notch.

Tate groaned and looked like he wanted to be anywhere but here.

"I'll see if one of the paramedics can come over," the female officer suggested, taking a large step away from me.

"Thanks." He gave her a dazzling smile, and for a microsecond, I forgot about the awful events that had happened.

Exhaling loudly, he then gave me a minute before attempting to bring the conversation back on task. "So, did you see anything suspicious at the time you found the body? Anyone hanging around that shouldn't have been there? Anything that looked out of place?"

I nodded.

"Okay." He half smiled. "Now we're getting somewhere."

I thought back over the moment I found Willow. Her unfocused eyes would haunt my dreams for a very long time. The way her neck was angled and the way her body lay; her shirt torn from the branches she had fallen on caused my heart to stop momentarily. But I'd kept my composure, and I'd tried to help her. I'd felt for a pulse and had wanted to give her CPR. Only it was clear that she was beyond my help, which is when I'd called for the paramedics and then ran back inside the hotel screaming.

"What did you see?" Tate gently pushed. "Was it someone you recognized?"

"Not someone."

He lifted an eyebrow,

"It was a squirrel." I hiccupped.

"A…" He froze. "A squirrel?"

"Uh-huh."

"Is that a nickname for someone you know?"

"Nope. It's a furry gray animal that lives in the wild."

"O… kay." Tate held the notebook and pen at the ready. However, he chose not to write that down.

"It's what made me notice Willow's leg. Sticking out from between the bushes," I finished. "Do you think she tripped over the branch?"

Tate closed the notebook, his shoulders dropping as he released a long breath. "No. We believe Willow fell from the window." I followed his finger as it pointed to the third-floor turret.

My stomach gripped in a wave of nausea, and I put my hand over my mouth to stop gagging. Tate's eyes widened, and he took a large step backwards.

"How?" I asked once I'd managed some self-control. "She was a smart woman. Surely, she knew better than to lean that far over the ledge? And besides, it's freezing today. Why would she even have the window open?"

"All very good questions that I'm trying to find the answers to. Now, did you hear anything from above that would indicate someone was in the room with her before the fall?"

"No!"

"And you didn't see anyone up there?"

"I didn't even look. Wait, are you suggesting that someone pushed Willow out the window?"

"I'm just gathering facts at this stage."

"Hang on a second." I lifted my hand, wanting to slow the pace. "You're a homicide detective, right?"

"Correct."

"Why are you here? Stoney Creek isn't big enough to have a homicide detective on staff, which means you've come from Snohomish. I know they have the services of the Sheriff's

Office Major Crimes Unit available to them. How did you get here so fast?"

Tate's brow furrowed as he took a slow breath and studied me. After a hesitant smile flashed, he gave a small nod of his head. "Very good. Now if we could get back to my questions. Did you see anything out of the ordinary?"

"No, I didn't. But you didn't answer my question—why are you here? I've done enough research to know you don't attend accidents unless you think there could be foul play involved."

"Miss Jackson..."

"Call me Aubrey."

He sighed. "Aubrey... I'm only investigating all angles."

I straightened my spine and sniffed loudly, considering his line of questioning. "You think she was murdered."

"Like I said, just gathering facts. Now, you've had a shock, and a paramedic will be with you shortly. It looks like your friends are waiting for you, so I'll leave the questioning until tomorrow. Please make yourself available." He nodded and spun on his heel, but before he stepped away, he looked back at me, and his eyes softened. "Aubrey, you've had a difficult afternoon. Take care of yourself tonight and surround yourself with loved ones. Seeing your first dead body is never easy."

* * *

Once Tate had moved to speak to Chris, and a paramedic had deemed I would be fine, I allowed Ellie and Spencer to lead me inside to the bar, where I was handed a large glass.

"I hate brandy," I moaned.

"I know," replied Ellie. "But it's good for you."

I narrowed my eyes. "Are you sure?"

"Uh-huh. Everybody knows that. Now come on, down it."

I gritted my teeth before doing as asked. The liquid burned the back of my throat, and I winced. "Geez." I coughed. "How can that be good for me?"

"I have no idea, but my grandpa always said it was, and I never argue with Grandpa. True, I'm not sure if the advice fits finding a dead body but better to play it safe." Ellie's eyes bulged as she scanned my face. "Do you feel better yet?"

I took a moment to consider my response. Admittedly, as the alcohol worked its way through my system, warming me up, I did start to feel calmer. "Maybe I should have another one."

Spencer lifted a finger in the direction of the bartender, and another glass miraculously appeared without any words being said.

Accepting the drink, I closed my eyes, parted my lips, and hurriedly swallowed the liquid before it could hit my tastebuds. However, it didn't stop the heat from hitting the roof of my mouth and oozing down my esophagus. My eyes watered, and my body shivered as a coughing fit took hold. I didn't consume a lot of alcohol, and I guessed it showed.

Spencer gently rubbed my back, which started a whole new load of emotions, and before I could stop it, tears once again flowed freely.

"Oh, Aubrey," he soothed, putting his arm around my shoulder and pulling me tightly against him.

I allowed myself a moment of enjoying his warmth, his steady heartbeat strong in my ear as his masculine scent did far more to soothe my nerves than the alcohol had. If he could bottle that and sell it to the mass market, Prozac would go out of business.

His lips gently grazed my forehead as he whispered, "It's going to be okay."

Was it? Certainly not for Willow.

Ellie handed me some napkins from the bar, and I managed to control my tears and slow my breathing, but I wasn't in a hurry to remove myself from Spencer's embrace. I'd never spent this long in his arms before, and it felt far too safe there.

"Come and sit near the fire," Ellie suggested, nodding to the vacant sofa. "The heat will help."

I wasn't so sure. Now that I had control of myself again, heat seemed to be radiating from me. True, that could have been from Spencer, or it could have been from the extra warm jacket I still had wrapped around me. I gasped as I grabbed at the fabric.

"I stole the detective's jacket. Oh my goodness! Does that make me a criminal?"

Ellie laughed as she led the way across the quiet room. "Don't stress. I'm sure he'll come looking for it."

Spencer quietly huffed, releasing his hold on me, and a coolness swept in.

I swallowed hard and followed them, finding a place on the sofa with my back against the armrest. This gave me a good view of the room and the man who had just entered, making a beeline for the bar.

"Who exactly is that guy?" I nodded toward the man I'd earlier seen in an altercation with Willow. At the time, he'd appeared intimidating whereas now he looked small, his shoulders rolled forwards as he accepted the glass from the bartender and drained the contents before asking for a second. If nothing else, sales of alcohol were skyrocketing.

"I believe that's Levi Jones," Ellie explained. "An ex-boyfriend of Willow's."

"I saw them earlier. It's what I was going to tell you about before we went back into our session."

Ellie's eyebrows shot north as I hurriedly brought them up-to-date with Willow's reaction to the man.

Spencer leaned in close. "Didn't you tell us that the police are investigating if Willow was pushed?"

I nodded as my stomach clenched. "That was the feeling I got from Detective Tate."

Spencer turned to look at Levi. "He seems more upset than most. In fact…. is he…"

"Oh the poor guy. He's sobbing." Ellie put a hand over her mouth. "Maybe we should ask him to join us. It's not nice to be alone at a time like this."

"Hang on a minute," I hissed, grabbing her arm. "I'm not sure how I feel about him."

Spencer sipped from his glass, his eyebrow cocked.

"Well, Willow didn't look happy to see him. If I'm correct, Spencer, you're suggesting that, if she was indeed pushed from the window, then there's every chance that he could be the pusher. If that's true, then do we really want to invite him over?"

"That's a pretty big assumption," Spencer muttered.

"Yeah, Aubrey," Ellie agreed. "Innocent until proven guilty, right? And besides, who knows what we may learn by chatting to him."

I bit my lip as Ellie squared her shoulders before standing and making her way toward Levi. He seemed shocked by her sudden appearance but hurriedly swiped at the moisture dripping from his chin and accepted her offer. As they stepped toward us, their voices carried forward.

"Do you have anyone you can call?" Ellie asked him. "Family staying with you?"

He shook his head. "No. I'm here alone. I've only just checked in. I wasn't going to stay, but after… Well, I want to be as close to Willow as I can." He sniffed loudly before swallowing the contents of his glass.

"Come and sit down here." Ellie led him to the armchair facing the sofa.

"Thank you. That's very kind of you." He placed his glass on the floor and slumped into the leather, his gaze roaming across Spencer and me. "I'm Levi. Levi Jones." He vigorously rubbed his thighs as he swallowed hard.

"Hi. I'm Spencer Stratford, and this is Aubrey Jackson."

"I'm sorry for your loss," I offered. The words were inadequate, but they were all I had.

"I—I can't believe she's gone." He rubbed the heel of his palm against his breastbone before tears once again filled his eyes. His hands then covered his face as he crumbled into himself. "What am I going to do without her?"

"Were you two an item?" A deep V formed between Ellie's brows as she gently held his forearm, crouching beside him.

"She was the love of my life," he whispered, more to himself than us.

My mind raced over the conversation I'd overheard between him and Willow, and I was unsure the feeling had been reciprocated.

"But I thought she was dating Jonathan Berkley?" Ellie gently poked.

"Wow! *The* Jonathan Berkley? The same guy that wrote the *New York Times* bestselling CIA operative suspense series?" I really needed to keep up with the gossip news.

"The *Mary Quinn Conspiracies* went viral," Spencer added. "And rightly so. They're some of the best books I've read." Ellie hurriedly nodded her agreement.

"The man's a hack," Levi spat, causing Ellie to jump and release her hold. "He can't write a thing."

I was sure Berkley's bank account begged to differ.

"And he didn't love her. Not like I do. She was just using him to get an introduction to Heron and Heron Publishing."

"Isn't she published with Blackwood and Finch?" Spencer asked.

"Yeah, but Heron just signed her latest novel. I've only read snippets, but I can tell you it's going to be the biggest book of the year." Levi stared into the distance.

"She got what she wanted then," I muttered to myself. Only the alcohol seemed to make my voice louder than normal as Levi's head snapped toward me, his eyes hard.

"Willow was a strong woman who made things happen. When she wanted something, nothing would stand in her way of getting it."

"So she left you for Berkley?" I pushed on, seemingly unable to control my mouth.

Levi flinched. "She was coming back to me. I just had to bide my time."

"But she had a restraining order against you!" Maybe it was the alcohol as I wasn't usually that outspoken. Two seconds after saying it, I wished I could retract it.

"How do you know about that?" Levi's eyes narrowed as he abruptly stood.

"Ummm… I just overheard it… somewhere." Not a complete lie.

Levi's eyes filled with tears, and his nostrils flared.

"That restraining order was done in a silly moment of misunderstanding. I strongly suggest for your own sake that you do not go around disclosing that kind of information." Heat flushed his face, and a storm brewed in his dark eyes as he pointed down at me.

Before I could reply, he turned sharply and stomped from the room, shoulder charging Nancy and knocking a bundle of notebooks from her hands. She death-stared after him, but thankfully Beverley helped her pick the mess up.

"Did he just threaten you?" Ellie asked as Spencer stiffened beside me.

"I'm sure he'll calm down." I hoped.

"His mood transformed quickly. No wonder Willow had a restraining order against him," Spencer mused. "Shame

Jonathan Berkley didn't get here in time. I'm sure he would have kept Levi away from her."

Just over a year ago, Ellie and I had first met Spencer at a multi-author book signing event at the Seattle Convention Center. Ellie had been there as a signing author, but as I'd still been unpublished at the time, I had gone along as her assistant for the day. Honestly, it had been super exciting being among eighty published authors and watching them greet their readers as they autographed their books inspired me to keep writing.

Spencer had been signing at the table alongside Ellie, and even though Berkley hadn't been there, the two of them had forged a friendship built on their love of his bestselling series. Me? I enjoyed Berkley's books and would love his success, but my favorite author was Gemma Halliday. If I ever met her, I think I'd faint.

"Jonathan Berkley is coming to this event?" I asked, surprised. "No wonder you two were so keen for this weekend!"

"Yeah. I told you about it last month," Ellie prompted.

"No, you didn't! Believe me I would have remembered."

Spencer shrugged. "I'd been hoping I could get some time with him and pick his brain about character development. Shame he pulled out last minute."

"No, I saw him! Only from a distance, but it counts, right?" Ellie sighed wistfully. "When we arrived this morning, I ducked down to the pond to take a selfie. An Uber pulled into the driveway, and I saw Berkley in the back."

"Are you sure it was him?"

Ellie nodded emphatically. "Positive. His jawline and raw sexuality are hard to dismiss." She'd always had a thing for strong men.

I rolled my eyes. "What if he saw Willow and Levi together?"

Spencer's jaw tensed. "Then I'd imagine he would have had a few harsh words with Levi. I know if Willow was my girlfriend, and someone was threatening her, I'd be overprotective and want him to stay away from her."

"But that's the thing. When I saw them in the room, Levi looked like he was scared of losing her."

"Do you think Levi was worried he'd lose her forever to Berkley and killed her in a fit of jealousy?" Ellie's eyes were bright as she leaned her elbows on her knees and placed her fists under her chin.

"That's quite the leap," Spencer scoffed.

"Maybe. But it's better than…" Her words drifted off as she pulled her shoulders back and looked anywhere but at us.

"What?" I asked. "What is it?"

"Nothing. It's nothing." Her eyes dulled as she waved her hand dismissively.

"Come on," I prodded. "I know you better than that."

Ellie huffed out a breath, her gaze darting around the room. When it settled on me, she leaned in close and whispered, "I hate to say this, but that detective sure seemed interested in Jenna."

"Jenna?"

"*Shhh!* Keep your voice down."

"Sorry, but what do you mean? How could you even think such a thing?"

"Well, Detective Tate kept asking me where she was at the time of death. As if I knew."

"She was in the bar with us," I commented.

"No, she wasn't," added Spencer. "She left with Ricky."

"What does it matter anyway?" I queried, dismissing the idea with the shake of my head.

Ellie shrugged. "I don't know, but the detective was super inquisitive."

"He asked me about her too," explained Spencer. "Asked what I thought of the relationship between her and Willow."

"What did you tell him?"

"Just that they were co-writers in a super successful series, and it was Jenna's idea to run this retreat together."

"But why do you think he's asking about her? He couldn't suspect her of anything." I spun the glass between my fingers, considering the implications of what they were suggesting.

"Don't they say money is at the root of everything?" Ellie added.

I raised my left eyebrow.

"Jenna and Willow's romance novel was very successful. There was a lot of money tied up between them," Spencer explained.

"And?" I stared at my friends, my eyes wide with disbelief.

"And money is usually the cause of most arguments."

"And murders," added Ellie quietly.

"You're not saying that Jenna hurt Willow over money, are you?" I almost choked on my drink.

"Of course not! But that doesn't mean the detective isn't considering it."

CHAPTER THREE

I sat up straight, my eyes wide as I stared at Ellie. "Look, we don't even know that Willow's death *wasn't* an accident."

"I know," she soothed. "I'm just letting you know what line of questioning the detective was taking."

My shoulders slumped as my thoughts scrambled. "How could he possibly think she's capable of such a thing? Jenna's the most loving, caring person you could ever ask to be friends with."

"Yeah, I know. But as a black belt in jujitsu she's a walking weapon."

"Well, that story's not exactly going to help me," Jenna interrupted, moving in behind the sofa and causing me to nearly jump out of my skin.

My hand flew to my heart as I stared up into her red-rimmed eyes. She looked pale; her mascara smudged beneath her lashes. Her shoulders sagged, her once neat shirt now hung untucked, and a vacant look filled her eyes.

Ellie leapt from her seat and pulled her in for a big hug. "Are you okay? Willow was your friend. You must be in shock."

Once Ellie had given her enough space to breathe, Jenna swiped at her tears. "I can't believe that she's gone. She was so vibrant and full of life. She worked hard and was so talented. You should read her next novel, *The Black Rose.* It'll blow your socks off! It has an ending that will break your heart yet yearn for a romance like it. Readers will love it… would've loved it," she finished quietly. "I guess no one will ever read it now."

Jenna dropped her head into her hands, and silent tears spilled between her fingers as Ellie led her to sit beside me.

"Maybe it'll still be published." I reached out and took her hand in mine, squeezing tightly. "Or maybe you could write something in your next book that honors her," I added, my heart breaking for my friend.

Jenna shook her head, using the back of her free hand to swipe at her cheeks. "The way the detective was treating me made my skin crawl. I believe he thinks I pushed her out the window."

"I'm sure he was just asking routine questions, and it'll turn out that Willow slipped and fell." Ellie's forehead wrinkled as she bit her bottom lip.

Jenna gulped. "I overheard the coroner telling the detective that there were scratches and bruises on her neck that were inconsistent with the fall."

"What does that even mean?" I asked.

"That someone possibly had their hands around her neck." Spencer shrugged.

"Okay, I'll concede that's a possibility. But what reason would Jenna have for wanting Willow dead?" I scoffed.

It was Jenna's turn to bite her lip, blinking back the tears as she stared hard at the floor.

"Jenna, what's wrong?" Ellie asked, placing her hand on Jenna's knee.

"Ummm, someone told the police that Willow and I were arguing last night, and it got quite heated."

"Were you?" I probed.

Jenna slowly nodded her head.

"Who would have told them that?"

"I think it was Nancy. She checked into the hotel yesterday because she'd booked her one-on-one time with Willow early."

"What were you arguing about?" Spencer asked.

Jenna crossed one ankle over the other as she shifted uncomfortably on the sofa, her hands wringing her fingers in knots. "Willow owed me a lot of money. From the sale of our book. She never paid me my share."

"Whoa. How much did she owe you?"

"Over one hundred thousand dollars."

"For one book?" I sucked in a fast breath. Those kinds of royalties weren't common for authors. To be in that league, you had to have a major bestseller on your hands. And to think that was only Jenna's half astounded me.

"Geez." Ellie sat back hard against the chair and released a slow whistle. "That's a lot of money."

"How could she not have paid you?" Spencer asked. "Surely you had a contract?"

"Of course! But our series was contracted between Willow and her agent, who sold the rights to the publisher Blackwood and Finch. My contribution was paid directly to me from Willow. I never liked the idea, but I didn't want to turn down an opportunity like that. Before meeting her I barely made a wage from my writing." She released a long breath and looked down at her hands. "I still feel like a fraud, that I'm not talented enough for her to have worked with me."

"Rubbish!" Ellie jumped in. "You're far more talented than she is. You deserved every bit of that fame and money."

Jenna gave a wry smile. "I was lucky, Ellie."

"Sure, you got a lucky break when you met her, but it was your ability and tenacity that made you a success."

"How did you meet her?" Spencer asked.

Jenna looked up at him, her eyes filled with a memory. "I was at a Romance Writers of America conference where I'd just won the RITA award for the best romance novel. Willow presented it to me, and afterwards at the awards dinner, we got chatting. She told me that she'd read my book and loved it and would I ever consider collaborating with her. I honestly couldn't believe my luck. I mean, who gets that kind of opportunity just handed to them?"

"You earned the RITA," I added. "That book was phenomenal. In my opinion, she was the lucky one."

"Yeah, well at first working with her was all sunshine and roses, but I quickly realized I was doing all the writing. Which I was fine with. She gave me the plot idea, and I fleshed it out. Of course, her name was the largest on the cover. She was already well-known. I completely understood, and after it was released and hit the *New York Times* bestseller list, I really didn't care who wrote what. The royalties were going to pay my mortgage for a long time and set up my own career. Only Willow controlled the purse strings, and she kept lying to me about when she was going to write the check. When she never did, I was angry with her because I really needed the money. But I didn't kill her for it. I was just going to get my lawyer to see to it once this retreat was over."

"Why did you do this retreat with her if she owed you so much money?"

Jenna slunk back in the chair. "When I first pitched her the idea for this weekend, she wasn't overly keen. But as time went by and she saw the business model that I proposed, she thought it would be good marketing for the hotel, and her attitude toward it changed. A lot. She started to talk about how we could take lots of photos of her teaching you all and saturate her social media platforms with them, and how inspired new authors would be to learn from her. At that time, I was asking her to pay me for the book we wrote, but she promised me that she would pay me everything I was owed as soon as the weekend started. Yet last night, she laughed when I asked for it again. Told me she'd pay it when she felt like it. Only my contract stipulates that I have to be paid within thirty days of her receiving the royalty check."

"And Detective Tate thinks you went back for another argument today and then pushed her out the window?"

Jenna shrugged. "He didn't say that exactly, but it felt that way."

"That's stupid. You're hardly going to get money from her now she's dead!" My eyes rolled so far into my head I felt woozy.

"He kept asking if I lose control of my emotions easily."

"Then that settles it. You're the most controlled person I know," I finished vehemently. "Jujitsu taught you that."

"I haven't done martial arts in years, Aubrey, and last night, I forgot all my training, and I did lose control of myself. You see, the bank is going to foreclose on my mortgage. I needed to be paid, and that money was mine! When she brushed me off as if it was nothing, I saw red."

"What exactly did you do?" Ellie asked, quietly.

"I threatened her. Told her I'd kill her if she didn't pay up. But I didn't mean it! It's just a saying. I say it to my cat every time he pees in my slipper. And he's still alive which proves I would never actually harm him."

"Except for that time you accidentally fed him too much shrimp and nearly poisoned him," I added.

"Aubrey! That's not helpful," Ellie barked.

"Sorry. But... you know. We need to be prepared in case the detective asks the vet about it. He looks very thorough. The detective that is. Not the vet."

Ellie shushed me with a glare.

"Okay. We need to ask around," continued Ellie leaning forwards. "See what we can learn. If we can figure this out, then the police have to leave you alone."

"We're not detectives, Ellie," Spencer warned.

"We're writers. Next best thing. Besides, Jenna needs our help," Ellie pushed. "She's our friend. We can't see her arrested for murder."

"She hasn't been arrested," Spencer pointed out. "She's barely been questioned!"

"I know. But even her being questioned could be the end of her career. It doesn't take long for the press to get their hands on a story like that."

"Readers are loyal," I reminded her.

"As she's the author of sweet romances, can you imagine what social media will do if she's arrested for a gruesome murder of her co-writer?"

She had a point.

Spencer sighed.

Jenna remained quiet.

"What would we even do?" I queried, hating the idea that the detective was even considering Jenna.

"We need to look at this as if we were writing a book. Plot it out and see where the case leads us."

"That's a good idea. But when we write a book, we carefully plan the murder. I don't think Willow's death worked that way," I explained.

"It doesn't matter! We have a victim and a list of suspects. We need to learn who had the means, motive, and opportunity." She counted off her fingers as she spoke.

"We have no suspects. We don't even know for sure that she *was* murdered," Spencer reminded her.

"True. But the police have reason to think she was. All we need to do is learn what the good detective knows." Ellie gave me a pointed stare.

"But the evidence won't point to Jenna as we all know that she didn't do it," I added, hugging my friend close.

"Sure, but it will be great practice for our next books. Come on, Aubrey. You were only just complaining to me about how you have writer's block. What could be better than investigating a real murder?"

Hmmm, the research would be invaluable.

"Oh great, so now we're solving murders as a cure for writer's block? Should I start worrying if you ever take up horror?" Spencer's brows were drawn together as he stared at me, and I couldn't tell if he was serious or not.

I playfully swatted his leg as a small thrill tickled my belly. I hoped it was because I was considering a real-life investigation and not because his eyes reminded me of a cloudless sky.

"We'd only be asking a few questions," Ellie continued. "It's not like we'll be doing the Jessica Fletcher thing where we investigate thoroughly."

That would be exciting though.

"Come on, Aubrey. It could be fun. And that super cute policeman was flirting with you, so you could easily get some answers from him."

"He wasn't flirting!" I surreptitiously eyed Spencer to gauge his reaction to that news. It was no secret that I had a massive crush on Spencer, but it was also no secret that he had no romantic interest in me. "And besides, if the detective really does consider Jenna, then he's no friend of mine."

"What you need to do is to tell him about Levi and what you saw earlier," Spencer added, his eyes locked onto mine.

I nodded. "Yeah, that's a good idea. But I don't have his number."

"You could always Google the number for the station and ask for him," Spencer explained.

"Nah." Ellie waved her hand dismissively. "He'll be back for his jacket. Tell him then."

"Would you all mind if I excuse myself and go to my room?" Jenna asked, standing. "My head is pounding, and I think a migraine might be starting. A rest may just cut it off before it takes hold."

"Do you want me to come with you?"

"Thanks, Aubrey, but I'll be fine. I know I have some Advil in my bag. I'll take some and try to get some sleep."

Thankfully, Jenna hadn't seen Willow lying in the bushes. Ellie had ensured that she'd been spared from that, which meant that Jenna may just be able to get that much needed sleep. Something I was sure would elude me when I finally made it to bed.

Jenna shuffled across the room, her head hung low, and her shoulders slumped. She appeared to have aged twenty years in only a few short hours.

"Poor thing. I feel so bad for her," Ellie whispered as we watched her leave.

"She's holding up pretty well," Spencer commented.

"Yeah, but don't be fooled. I know her well enough to know that on the inside her heart is breaking." My own heart cracked thinking about it.

As Jenna exited the room, Chris entered, announcing if anyone was hungry that dinner was served in the dining room. Dark rings lined his eyes, and his skin looked sallow as fatigue weighed his shoulders down.

"I know it's a few hours late, and you're probably not hungry, but the chef has served it regardless."

Spencer stood, rubbing his stomach. "Are you coming?"

"How can you eat at a time like this?" Ellie asked.

He shrugged. "To be honest, I didn't know Willow on a personal level. Today was the first time I'd met her, and as much as I'm sad that a life has been lost, my stomach is rumbling."

Couldn't argue with that I guess.

* * *

My stomach wasn't made of the same stuff that Spencer's was, so instead of going for dinner, I excused myself and went to my room for a shower.

The ensuite wasn't large, but it was modernized and had everything I needed. The pedestal sink and over-the-bath shower were reminiscent of Victorian times, but the dark blue walls and checkered tiled floor gave it a more modern feel.

Pulling back the white shower curtain, I dropped my clothes on the floor and stepped in, turning the water to steaming. I wasn't sure how long I allowed the water to soothe me, but it wasn't long enough to wash the thought of Willow from my mind. Once the hot water turned to cold, I shut off the taps, wrapped myself in the sumptuous towel, and went in search of my pink striped pajamas. Emily used to tease me for being a girly-girl for my love of pink, but I'd often fought back, stating I loved purple just as much.

Slipping my feet into my fluffy slippers, I sank onto the bed and sent a text message to my mom, telling her about the start to the retreat. Exhaustion filled every cell of my body, yet my mind was whirling at a thousand miles an hour.

This morning, I'd been filled with excitement to get some work done, to learn from the talented Willow Fox, and I couldn't wait for my one-on-one session with her to help with my writer's block. Not even for a millisecond did I ever think the day could have turned so badly. Spencer's cautionary words about her death being an accident played through my mind, and I allowed myself to be comforted by the thought.

But what had made Willow go to her room when she was supposed to be standing in front of a group of authors giving us a lecture on how to write compelling characters? She'd spent a good hour this morning telling us that we had to take our work seriously and to commit ourselves to the job. Surely, she would heed her own rules and be punctual for our session?

Thinking back, I guess she had been pretty shaken after her run in with Levi. Maybe she'd just popped upstairs to compose herself before meeting us all again.

Earlier when Detective Tate had pointed to the third-floor turret, showing me where he believed Willow to have fallen from, I'd known it was the room above mine. She would have fallen directly past my window. Curious, I stood and moved to it, lifting the old latch and pushing it open. The cold night air blew in the earthy scent of the evergreen trees, the evening silence palpable, and I shivered against it.

Hmmm, the window opening was low, but it wasn't really that wide. Was the turret window the same? I held the frame tight as I turned to look up, noting the stars dotting the night sky, the turret reaching eerily into the darkness. Three stories wasn't that high, and as much as I was sure the landing would have hurt, surely Willow could have survived the fall. I mean, if I had accidentally slipped, I would have been grasping for the ledge, trying to slow myself down. And surely, she could have used her legs to have caught the window frame? Of course, everything would have been happening quickly, not giving her much time to think, but fight-or-flight kicks in, right? And that would have had her reacting to the situation.

The memory of her body swam in front of me. The vacant look in her eyes, her dark hair splayed around her, twigs and leaves intermingled with their lustrous stands. I remembered the rips to her shirt caused by the branches, but I didn't recall any on her pants. Would they have caught on the window frame if she'd tried to stop her fall?

Pulling myself back inside I allowed my fingers to trail their way around my window, noting the old wood, rough with age. The metal catch had sharp edges, and hinges were rusted from the seasons. If the upstairs room was the same as this one, for sure Willow's clothing would have shown the signs. I turned to look at the garden below, but in the darkness the shadows looked eerie.

Hurriedly reaching for my phone, I flipped on the flashlight and aimed it toward the ground, allowing it to illuminate the broken shrubs where Willow had landed.

But hang on. Willow was lying on the ground face up. If she'd accidentally slipped, she would have been lying face down. Unless she was sitting on the open window ledge facing into the room. But who would do such a stupid thing? Willow was an intelligent woman. She would have known better. I felt uneasy just leaning out the window, let alone sitting with my back to the drop.

Shivering, I moved to close the window when my phone slipped from my fingers and fell the two stories to the ground. My squeal mingled with the soft sound of leaves rustling, and my phone died in the darkness. My heart sank.

Geez, Aubrey! Now you have to go out into the dark cold night, with no flashlight, to find your phone. What the heck is wrong with you?

Hurriedly closing the latch, I swapped my slippers for my boots and grabbed my jacket. My door creaked closed behind me as the echoes of the night danced along the empty hallway. Distant sounds of televisions drifted under doorframes as I moved past them, and for a brief moment, I wished that the only concern I had tonight was what was happening in the latest episode of *The Kardashians*. If I'd been minding my own business, that's exactly what I would have been watching.

But then Jenna's distraught eyes flashed in my mind, and I knew I'd been doing the right thing. Willow's fall could have been an accident, but there were a few questions that needed to be answered.

My boots padded softly against the carpet runner lining the stairs but clunked as I stepped onto the wood floorboards that covered the common areas of the ground floor. Chris had locked everything up for the night, with only skirting board lights glimmering a path to the front door. An oak grandfather clock ticked in the nearest room, and I flinched as a door hinge squeaked behind me. I gasped and spun to see who was there. Shadows flickered, and I could have sworn the sound of ghosts echoed over my shoulder. The mansion was a lot eerier at night than it was during the day, and I was now positive this one was haunted.

Tucking my jacket tighter around my neck, I hurriedly unlocked the front door, jumping at the loud clunk. Somehow it felt safer outside, where I could follow the soft garden lighting along the path that surrounded the house, stopping below my window. Thankfully, I'd left my curtains open which meant it was easy to spot which room was mine. Now all I had to do was locate my phone in the dark bushes.

I sighed. Why hadn't I knocked on Ellie's door and asked her to come with me? Better yet, I could have rallied Spencer's help. But then I would have had to admit how clumsy I'd been. Yeah, best I left that one alone.

The nearest path light showed me the broken bushes where Willow had lain. The wind picked up rustling the leaves in the trees, and I could have sworn Willow just whispered in my ear. I shivered.

"Hey, Willow, if your spirit's still around, please don't scare me. I just want to find my phone, okay? In fact, a bit of help would be appreciated." After Emily had passed, I'd spent a lot of time researching the afterlife, having readings from mediums, and filling my houseboat with crystals that would enhance my own psychic abilities. I liked the idea that she could still communicate with me and soon learned that spirits would speak to us in many different ways—flickering lights, random feathers, and sudden drops in temperature were just a few.

After a moment of none of these, I figured I was on my own. Which was great because as much as I was happy to chat to

Emily—and maybe Willow—unknown ghosts were a whole different ball game.

"All right, Aubrey. Stop procrastinating and just do it." Hearing my own voice settled my nerves slightly, giving me the push I needed to get the job done. Dropping to the ground, I ran my hands through the fallen leaves, a broken branch scratching my wrist. The earthy smell of decomposing leaves and animal poop clogged my sinuses, and I sneezed against it. The sudden noise scared a squirrel, and it ran up my arm and over my back before I could scream loud enough to scare it away. Geez, I hated nature. In the dark. Alone. How much did I really want to find this phone?

"You know, Willow, I'm only trying to solve what happened to you. Can you please give me a helping hand?"

Willow's spirit either heard me and wanted to help, or wanted to get rid of me, because at that moment, a glorious tinkle alerted me to a text message, and my phone screen lit up like a Christmas tree.

Thank the Lord above.

It was located a few feet away from my search area, which meant I had to lean farther into the bushes to grab it. Once my fingers were clutched around it, I noted the time. Eleven past eleven. Eleven, eleven. Angel numbers. A flutter of excitement stirred in my belly with the reassurance I was on the right path and exactly where I was meant to be. After all, angels wouldn't bother if I was on the wrong path, right?

I flipped the flashlight on and sank back on my heels, grateful for the light and how it gave me a feeling of safety. I basked in that glow all too quickly though as, at that moment, another squirrel jumped from a fallen nest and scurried away from me. I liked squirrels. I really did, only not when I was sitting amongst dead leaves in the dark of night, alone.

Taking a few slow breaths, my heart rate dropped back into normal range as my light flashed over the nest, searching for any other creatures that may jump out at me. Thankfully, it all looked empty but sympathy for the little creatures that had taken the time to build their now broken home sat heavy in my belly. They really were the masters of repurposing rubbish. Discarded leaves, twigs, a few feathers, and shredded bark intermingled with discarded paper and pine needles. But hang on. On closer inspection, the paper didn't belong. It was far too clean and wasn't crumpled into the mess like everything else was. No, it looked more like a squirrel had just dropped it.

Something about the paper caught my attention, and I flashed my light over it, wanting a closer look. The lined page was filled with flowery handwriting now difficult to read as the damp night air had seeped into the page. Carefully removing it from its resting place, I tried to read what the words were, only it was far too difficult in this light. Flicking the dirt from it, I pushed it into my jacket pocket and stood, ready to make my way back to my room and another shower before bed.

The text message that had saved my phone shone brightly on the screen, and I took a moment to read who it was from.

Aubrey, stay safe. I don't want to lose two girls. Love Mom x

I sighed, Mom's anxiety causing my heart to hurt. It was stupid to be out here alone at night, and I needed to be more sensible. A murderer could be amongst us, and who knew if Willow was the only person they wanted dead?

Okay, my imagination was running in overdrive, and the thoughts were not very reassuring. And they definitely wouldn't help me sleep tonight.

Scurrying as fast as my feet would allow, I made my way back to the safety of my room.

* * *

Saltwater Bay had a very small police department that answered the call of duty no matter the time of day or night. One sergeant and one officer. When things got serious they borrowed a detective from St. Thomas.

"So… where's the rest of him?" I asked, my entire body shaking. After my knees had given out and I'd felt the world sway, Grayson had steadied me and helped me to sit down. But that had only placed me at eye level with the remains, which in turn had started my stomach convulsing. By the time the police had arrived, the area around the beach house looked a whole lot worse.

Officer Oliver Winston lifted his cap and swiped his forehead as a trickle of perspiration ran down his temple. "If it's even male, I'm guessing out there somewhere." He glanced *toward the ocean glistening in the sunlight. Oliver was a bit younger than I was and a complete cutie pie. If you were into skinny blond guys with a heart of gold, that was.*

"It's male." *At six-foot-three, Sergeant Keagan Murphy stood ramrod straight, his uncompromising attitude and single nod of the head daring anyone to argue with him.* "That's Jenkins Butler."

Oliver's eyes widened, a look of reverence lurking in their gray depths. "How can you deduce that from a skull?"

I too was curious about the answer to that.

"The gold-capped tooth. Not too many people have those these days."

Oliver gasped.

A memory sparked in the back of my mind. "Where do I know that name from?" *I asked, daring to test my rubbery legs.*

Grayson took my hand as I pushed up from the ground. I was startled by his touch, and he hurriedly let go.

"Have you been to the caves outside of town?" *Keagan asked, ignoring Grayson. The two had a history that had led to a mutual dislike for each other. I didn't know the details as Gray always clammed up whenever I probed him about it, and I definitely wasn't interrogating a police officer to get the truth. Nope, Bernie always said if it didn't concern you, then it's best to stay out of it. Great advice to live by.*

"Yeah, I've done the tours heaps of times," *I replied.*

"Then you would've seen the plaque we erected for Jenkins Butler. He was the local expert who disappeared inside the caves two years ago. To this day, I don't know how, as he knew those systems like the back of his hand. His home was filled with maps and charts of the caverns, but even after we used every resource we could find, his body was never recovered."

Sadness weighed on my heart.

Oliver turned toward the skull, his forehead a bevy of deep lines. "That's your only unsolved case, isn't it, Sarg?"

Keagan scratched his chin as he looked into the distance. "Yeah. And it didn't sit well with me. We brought in cave experts to help us navigate the passages, thinking there must be a place where he'd got stuck. But nope. As far as we all could tell, he was nowhere to be seen."

The mystery was folklore around town, and I had vivid memories of overhearing Grandma Bernie talking to her best friend Maeve about it. A man had entered the caves and never returned. Caves which had only one way in and one way out. It had given me nightmares for weeks, and after that, I would never enter the caves alone.

"So how did his skull end up under my house?" I asked.

Grayson remained silent as he took a step backwards, yet I could see his thoughts whirling through his mind.

Keagan released a long, slow breath. "Once the forensic team and detectives arrive from St Thomas, I'm hoping we'll have the answers to that." *He looked at his watch.* "The boat should be here in the next forty minutes."

"What's your guess as to what happened?" *Oliver asked him.*

Keagan lowered his brow, turning his attention back to the skull. "There was a cavern that we didn't find, and his body has been lost to it. With the storm last night, it's very possible the copious amounts of water that flowed through the cave system has dislodged it from wherever it's been stuck and washed it out to the ocean."

"That's so sad," *I mused.* "Do you think maybe he had a heart attack and died with no one to help him?"

Keagan turned to me, his thick black brow drawn so low I could barely see his eyes. "No. The gaping big hole in the back of his skull tells me that he was murdered."

After making it back to my room, I'd studied the ripped paper to see what clues it may hold. Only the page was too damp to make out the words properly, so I dropped it onto the small desk to wait for it to dry. Then I'd found my laptop and disappeared with Daphne for a while. I needed an escape from the real world, and Saltwater Bay was a fun place to be.

Writing came naturally to me but often could be unpredictable. Sometimes I found a blank page terrifying, but sometimes in the most unexpected moments, the worlds I created appeared effortlessly. Tonight, it seemed this retreat was doing what I'd hoped it would do. The writer's block was fading. Words were starting to flow once again. Which in turn seemed to make me hungry.

As I stood and shook the cramps from my legs, I realized that I'd been lost in my fictional world for quite a few hours. It was now two a.m., and thoughts of missed dinner danced in my mind. I was considering popping down to the kitchen in search of food, but my thoughts were suddenly halted as I heard floorboards in the room overhead creak. My gaze shot upwards, and I froze as the eerie sound moved across the ceiling, every groan of the wood loud in the silent night air.

Someone was in Willow's room.

CHAPTER FOUR

———

My heart missed several beats as my thoughts raced. Who would be there at this time of the morning? What were they looking for? Was it the killer returning to remove some evidence? Or was it a grieving friend wanting to be close to a lost loved one? I knew the room had police tape across the door as they considered it part of the crime scene, so no one should be up there.

"Stop it, Aubrey. It could be anyone! In fact, it's probably just the old building moving from the cold air."

I relaxed my shoulders but squelched a scream as a loud *thump* and the sound of shattered glass shook the ceiling above my head. I held my breath through the moments of silence before the sound of hurried footsteps retraced their way to where they started.

Whoever was there was getting out fast. I didn't know the layout of the hotel that well, but I'd been enthralled by the old drawings of the building that were framed in the library, and if my memory was correct, the only room up there was the turret room. That meant whoever it was would have to come down the stairs.

Curiosity had me questioning who and why and if it was connected to Willow's death. After all, it was a room that no one should be in. Making the quick decision, I slipped my feet into my slippers and rushed to open my bedroom door.

Old mansions made a lot of noise in the dead of night, and as I tiptoed along the hallway toward the stairs, the idea that a killer could be among us suddenly made this feel like a bad idea. But I'd never done anything to make someone want to kill me, so surely I was safe. And if I bumped into the culprit, I already had my excuse ready. I was heading to the kitchen to settle my grumbling belly.

The overhead stairs groaned, so I picked up my pace, hoping to see who it was, but by the time I rounded the corner, the staircase that led up to the turret was empty.

I found a light switch and flipped it up, blinking against the glare of the overhead bulbs. Spinning in circles, I saw no one. How? Where did they go? And how had I missed seeing them? Well, that was weird. Had they been fast enough to make it to the ground floor before I caught them?

Making a hasty decision, I hugged my arms tight against my body and slowly ascended the stairs, wincing with every creak and groan they made. At the top, I was surprised to find only a small landing, approximately four feet square, with two doors. One was Willow's room crossed over with police tape, but another smaller version sat opposite it.

My heart beat fast as I reached out to the handle, unsure of what was on the other side. I held my breath and turned the knob, ready for anyone who may jump out at me. Thankfully, the only thing behind it was a pile of boxes and an old broom. It was nothing but a storage closet.

A breeze pulled me from my thoughts, and a feeling I was being watched made me shiver as a shadow caught the corner of my eye. Spinning to see who it was, I noted the stairwell was empty.

Oh geez. Was Willow's soul now lost and roaming the building, searching for who killed her? Would she be here forever if we didn't learn the truth? Or would she just start knocking things over until someone paid attention and solved the case?

I shivered. Way too many questions that I had absolutely no answer to. Rubbing my goosebumps away, I took the stairs two at a time and allowed the light spilling up toward me from the downstairs to guide me to the kitchen, my hearing on high alert for anything that would tell me where the mystery person had gone. But all I heard was the soft voice of Naomi drifting on the still night air. Had she been the one on the stairs?

Stepping up to the kitchen doorway, I saw her sitting casually on a chair tucked up to the table, her breathing unlabored. I highly doubted she'd been the owner of the racing footsteps.

"Everything will be okay now." Her voice was low and quiet as she talked into her phone. "Of course no one saw me! Do you think I'm an idiot?"

The old board beneath my step protested with my weight, and Naomi snapped her head around, her pale skin flushing with color as she hurriedly said her goodbyes to whoever was on the other end of the call.

"Sorry," I commented moving into the room. "I didn't mean to startle you. To be honest, I didn't expect anyone to be awake." My gaze rapidly scanned for who might have been making a hasty escape. "Did anyone else just come through here?"

Her brow furrowed as she absently tucked her blonde, bobbed hair behind her ear. "No. Just me. I was just talking to... ummm, my mom. Telling her about this afternoon."

I knew my mom wouldn't be happy if I called her after midnight, but then the death of a friend probably would soften her.

"I'm so sorry for your loss, Naomi. I'm sure Willow was more than your boss. As her assistant, you must have been very close."

"Yes." She lifted her heart-shaped face, her large brown eyes hard as they locked on to mine. "It's all so tragic. And we were... very close. Very, very close. I'm devastated."

I guessed not everyone showed grief with their tears.

"Would you like a hot drink?" I asked, moving across the black and white checkered tiled floor toward the kettle. The room looked like it had recently been refurbished with the cream-colored cabinets topped with highly polished marble. The appliances were sleek stainless steel, and the enormous oak table in the center of the room looked inviting.

"No thank you." She lifted a glass of wine, nodding toward the bottle alongside her. "What are you doing up at this time of night?"

"I couldn't sleep, and once I realized I missed dinner, there was no way my stomach was going to wait until the morning." For some reason, I felt compelled to keep what I'd heard to myself.

"There's cake in the refrigerator if you want something sweet."

Now she was speaking my language.

"I'm guessing you couldn't sleep either." I found the dessert she was talking about and helped myself to a large slice of chocolate heaven.

"Too much on my mind."

"I guess you lost a job as well as a friend. What do you think you'll do now?"

"Honestly, Aubrey, I have no idea!"

"Sorry."

"So you keep saying."

Behind me, the floor emitted a creak, prompting me to glance over my shoulder. In the doorway stood Ellie, her eyes wide as she shifted her gaze between us.

"Oh! I didn't expect anyone to be up," she said as she tightened her long knit sweater over her pajamas. "I couldn't sleep and thought a hot cup of cocoa would help. Is that cake for anyone?"

"Sure. It won't help our insomnia though," I replied, grateful to have someone to break the tension building around Naomi. Not that I blamed her, but it wasn't something I wanted to deal with in the middle of the night.

"Can I have a piece too?" Spencer moved in behind Ellie, and my mouth suddenly dried. His striped, long pajama pants were coupled with a Rangers hoodie. A five o'clock shadow grazed his chin, and dark-rimmed eyes made him look vulnerable. It took everything I had not to rush toward him and give him a hug.

"Is anyone in this house asleep?" I asked, fighting my urges and cutting him a slice.

"Yeah, Beverley is. I can hear her snoring through the walls. For a moment there, I thought she was auditioning for the Chainsaw Massacre sequel." Spencer grimaced.

"Is that what that noise was?" Ellie moved into the room and accepted the plate I held out to her, before passing one to Spencer.

"Cocoa?" I asked, finding cups in the overhead cupboards.

"Yes please," Ellie and Spencer said in unison. They grinned at each other and then sat opposite Naomi at the table.

Naomi's face flushed as she averted her gaze toward her glass of wine. Taking a large swig, she then pinned Spencer with a glare.

"Spencer, at the afternoon break, did I see you speaking to Ricky Campbell?"

With everything that had happened, I'd almost forgotten Ricky had been escorted off the premises by Jenna.

"Ah, yeah. Before our last session."

"What did he want? Did he say why he was here? What was he talking to you about?"

Spencer shook his head. "Not much really. He mostly spoke about a plot he had for a new series about a young girl who gets kidnapped by her father and given a new identity. Years later, she's working for the CIA when she stumbles across the truth of who she really was. It sounded really interesting."

"That was all?" Naomi pushed, the pitch of her voice increasing an octave. "Surely he didn't come here to chat about a book he hasn't written yet." She spun the stem of her wine glass between her fingers.

Spencer shrugged. "He said he was upset because Willow wouldn't take his calls, but he didn't say why."

"Is that why he came?" I asked, making our drinks and moving them to the table. "To speak to Willow in person?"

"Possibly," Spencer said, accepting his mug.

You could practically see the cogs turning in Naomi's mind.

"Do you think he had anything to do with her death?" Ellie asked.

Naomi stiffened.

"Why would you think that?" I asked Ellie, sliding a cup toward her.

"He wasn't on the guest list, right? And did you know that in his last thriller novel the victim was murdered by being pushed out of a window?"

I gasped.

Naomi ground her teeth.

"Hmmm, that's true," Spencer added. "What was it called again?" His fingers drummed against the wood tabletop.

"*Death in the Country*," Ellie supplied. "It was a good book. They only found the murderer after a hair sample was found at the crime scene. Such a great twist at the end too."

"Yeah, I wish I'd thought of it," added Spencer.

Naomi placed her hands on the table as she scraped her chair backwards and stood hurriedly. Snatching the half empty bottle of wine and her glass, she snarled, "If you'll all excuse me, I'm going to bed." Her shoulders were rigid as she stomped from the room, disappearing into the darkness.

Ellie cringed. "That was pretty insensitive of me to speak about Willow around her. I should have thought about her feelings."

"Don't be so quick to judge yourself Ellie," Spencer offered. "I wasn't completely honest before when I told her Ricky hadn't mentioned why he was upset."

I placed my elbows on the table and leaned forward. "So why was he?"

"He said he *needed* to speak to Willow. Emphasis on the word needed."

I raised an eyebrow.

"I don't know why exactly, but he kept muttering something about Naomi getting the sack once the retreat was over."

"How would he know that?" I asked.

Spencer shrugged. "Jenna got to him before he could tell me."

"A better question is, where did he go once he left?" Ellie mused, staring into her mug.

"What are you thinking?"

"That maybe he didn't leave and instead popped upstairs to talk to Willow about whatever *it* was, things got heated, and he pushed her out the window."

Spencer scratched the smattering of whiskers that peppered his chin. "What's his motive, though?"

"He seemed pretty steamed when Jenna led him from the room," Ellie added. "Whatever he needed to speak to Willow about had him worked up."

"Okay, let's assume for a minute that he hung around," Spencer suggested. "How did he know which room was Willow's?"

"He could have followed her," I added.

"Good point. But how did he get her to open the window?"

"Maybe he opened it," Ellie mused, her fork full of cake stopping halfway to her lips.

"That would make the murder premeditated." I sat up straight.

"What we need to do next is to ask Jenna if she could verify if Ricky left the grounds or not." Ellie dropped the fork onto her plate and pulled her phone from the pocket of her sweater, opened her notes app, and started to tap at the screen. "Okay, job number one is to speak to Jenna in the morning."

"We also need to add Jonathan Berkley to our list," Spencer added, before filling his fork with cake.

"Why?" It was late, and my brain was having a hard time keeping the pieces in play.

"Well, where is he? I know the man's a genius and my literary hero, but don't you think it's strange that he hasn't been seen or heard of since Willow's death? If it were my girlfriend, you'd hear my grief on the other side of town." Spencer's brow was pulled low, the stark overhead lighting causing his lashes to shadow on his cheeks.

"Unless it was him I heard in Willow's room just now." My finger traced the rim of the mug.

Both Ellie and Spencer stared at me, their eyes wide.

I hurriedly brought them up-to-date with my two a.m. escapades.

"Are you sure it was footsteps you heard?" Ellie asked, placing her phone on the table.

"Positive. I rushed to the stairs to see who it was, but despite the fact I could still hear steps, I couldn't see anyone there."

Spencer finished the last mouthful of cake, a crease in his brow forming as he got lost in thought.

"Do you think it was Naomi?" Ellie asked. "You said she was in the kitchen when you got here."

I shook my head. "I wondered the same thing, but when I came in she didn't look like she'd hurriedly sat down. She looked more like she'd been involved in a deep and meaningful conversation with whoever was on the other end of the phone." I retold the story of the conversation I'd overheard between her and her mom.

"Naomi might have known that Willow was going to sack her," Spencer mused. "They could have argued about it, and she could have pushed her in a temper."

"But Naomi being the killer doesn't make sense," said Ellie, tapping away at her phone screen. "If she killed Willow, she was out of a job anyway."

"True. But she doesn't look overly upset about her passing, does she?" I shrugged.

"Aubrey!" Ellie swatted my arm. "Everyone grieves differently."

"I know. I know." I swallowed hard, pushing a familiar feeling back down into my stomach. "But I still think you should add her to the list of suspects. After all, we don't know why Willow was going to sack her. She could have been up to anything. And despite the fact I don't think she could have been the one I heard in Willow's room just now, she was the one I found wide awake."

* * *

By the time the clock struck six a.m., I'd had exactly two hours sleep. And I didn't function well without a good eight hours. I did manage to pull on jeans and my powder blue fluffy sweater with the scalloped neckline. It accentuated my gold necklace with the amethyst heart that Emily had given me, and I took a minute to hold the stone tight within my palm and try to feel a connection.

Since her passing, all I really felt was sadness when I thought of her. I told my therapist it was like shallow breathing. I'd go about my day smiling with my friends and enjoying the moment, only the feeling stayed high in my body and didn't go all the way to my soul. But this morning, I was tired, and I craved to feel her close despite the pain the memories caused.

I squeezed my eyelids shut as my fingers traced the edges of the pendant, the cool stone warming against my touch. "Emily, are you here? Can you send me a sign if you are?"

My hearing sharpened as I waited for her to speak in my ear.

Only nothing. Just the faint hum of the heater and the distant rustling of leaves as the wind whipped the trees.

I swallowed down my disappointment and busied myself applying minimal makeup to cover the baggage sitting under my eyes then pulled my long hair into a ponytail. Once I was happy that was the best it was going to be today, I made my way down to the dining room, the aroma of coffee guiding my way.

Entering the room, I stopped in front of the buffet table and inhaled deeply, my tired brain instantly soothed. The smell of warm croissants competed with the fresh bread, which was overshadowed by the bacon, sausage, and eggs. The Bircher muesli looked good alongside the dish of fresh fruits, and I poured a glass of cranberry juice as I debated whether to go straight to the coffee or have the apple Danish first. Only before I could decide, I crossed paths with Nancy.

"Oh dear." She grimaced, her gaze rapidly roaming my body.

"Good morning," I returned, mustering my biggest smile.

"Is it?" She looked doubtful as she considered my appearance.

"The jury's still out, but I'm trying my best," I returned, ignoring her disapproving glance.

She patted my arm sympathetically before helping herself to a breakfast bagel and putting as much distance between us that she could. Couldn't say I was unhappy about that.

"Aubrey!" Ellie hissed as she hurried toward me. "He's here."

"Huh?"

"Detective Tate. And he's looking for you. Remember what we spoke about last night. Get as much information from him as you can." I had no idea how she looked so perky when her total hours of sleep couldn't have been much more than mine. "And maybe just… ummm, wake up a bit."

"I need coffee before I can do that," I groaned, eyeing a bacon and egg muffin that was calling to me.

"Good morning, Aubrey." A slightly familiar baritone called my name, and I spun to see Detective Tate silhouetted against the morning sun shining through the window. I blinked against the glare, and as he came into focus, I lost all train of thought.

"How does everyone look so damned good on only a few hours of sleep?" I mumbled, noting his damp hair brushed neatly back and cleanly shaven face. This morning, he wore well-loved jeans, a black T-shirt and a wool-lined brown jacket left open, so I had a great view of the badge attached to his belt.

"Pardon?"

"Ummm, I was just saying how much I really need coffee."

"Then let me help you with that." His long arms reached across the table and collected two mugs. Expertly filling them, he smiled, and the muffin I'd been considering was long forgotten.

"Remember what I said," Ellie whispered in my ear. "Pry him for information."

"Do you mind if we sit and chat?" he asked.

"Sure, but I won't be much help until I've had at least two of those." I nodded toward the cup he was holding out to me.

"I can arrange that." He smiled, and I enjoyed the view as his denim clad butt sauntered across the room to a quiet table tucked into the bay window. It was his enquiring glance in my direction that broke me from the trance he'd cast.

Good God, Aubrey. Get a grip.

Hurrying after him, I pulled out a chair and sat down, rolling my shoulders to relieve some of the tension already building.

"Trouble sleeping?" he inquired, picking up a sugar packet from the little glass jar on the table.

"Yeah. Just couldn't shake the look in Willow's eyes from my mind."

"I'm sorry you had to witness that."

"How do you do it? As a homicide detective, you must see your fair share of dead bodies."

He nodded, ripping the sugar packet open and emptying it into his cup. "Since I've relocated, the count has slowed. Thankfully."

"Where were you before here?"

"New York."

"Quite the change. What made you move?"

Stirring his coffee, his eyes clouded. He took a moment before clearing his throat and lifting his eyes to mine. "It *is* quite the change, but one that I'm enjoying so far."

I noticed he avoided my query.

"Now, Aubrey, I hope you're feeling up to answering a few more questions about what you saw yesterday."

I nodded and poured three sugars into my cup. This morning, I needed the boost.

He opened his notebook and flipped a few pages, only stopping once he'd found what he was looking for. I glanced over and saw my name underlined twice. Not much was written beneath it.

"Can you please recall everything you remember?" Tate prompted.

My hand shook as I stirred the black liquid and took a deep breath. "It's weird that throughout the night all I could see in my mind was Willow's body, and this morning, everything but that feels blurry."

"It's common when you've had a shock. Often details will reveal themselves once you've had some time. I noticed you stayed here last night and didn't return home."

"I thought about going home but decided I wanted to be with my friends. Many of the other authors at the retreat also stayed. I think they'll head home today though. At least I will. Detective, did you know that Ricky had written a book where the victim was murdered by being pushed out of a window?"

"Ricky?" he flipped the pages of the notebook backwards and forwards.

"Ricky Campbell."

"I don't recall his name being on the list of attendants."

"That's because he wasn't invited. In fact, Willow didn't want him here." I filled in the details about how Ricky had been escorted off the property.

"Do you know why?"

I shook my head. "Spencer was the one who spoke to him."

"I'll make a note to talk to Spencer. Did you ever see anyone showing Willow unwanted attention?"

"In what way?"

"Anyone ever hang around her when she wasn't looking? That kind of thing?"

"That's creepy."

"Exactly."

"Are you saying she had a stalker?" I liked that idea a heck of a lot more than Jenna being the prime suspect.

"I'm not saying anything. At this stage, I'm just covering all possibilities." Tate's smoke gray eyes locked on to mine, and heat crept its way up my neck.

"There was Levi," I croaked, willing the heat to dissipate and not to embarrass myself. I mean, the detective was very good-looking, but I'd seen my share of good-looking men, so why was he affecting me this way? Could it have anything to do with the air of authority and safety that surrounded him?

"Levi Jones?"

I mentally shook myself and refocused on the case at hand. "Uh-huh. I believe he's an ex of Willow's."

"He was here yesterday?"

"Yep. I overheard Willow telling him he wasn't supposed to be because of the restraining order. We spoke to him afterwards though, and he seemed genuinely upset."

Tate didn't comment, instead scribbled some illegible notes in his book.

"Don't the police have more digitized notebooks these days?" I asked.

Tate paused and glanced up at me.

I gulped. "I have a friend who works for the department, and she keeps me current with procedures and things like that."

"So I've heard."

"You've heard about the digital notebooks or my friend?"

"Both." A muscle near his jaw twitched.

Oh geez. "So why don't you use the digital notepad?"

"Not everyone likes technology." He studied me for a beat, his gaze sharp. "You ask a lot of questions."

"It's important that I get the facts right to keep my books believable."

Tate nodded, his gaze intent as he stared at me. "You want to keep them believable? Then you'd better ensure your good-looking female *amateur* sleuth who takes it upon herself to investigate the crime, without a doubt putting herself in danger, stays out of it this time."

"What are you insinuating?" I bit my lip. "That I'll stick my nose in where it doesn't belong?"

"If my research is correct," he countered, the corners of his lips twitching upwards, "that's what the heroine always does."

"So, you've read a lot of mysteries?"

He shrugged. "When I'm investigating a crime surrounding a group of writers, I like to keep up with my research."

"Good to know. Because if you're as thorough as I think you are, then my friend Jenna will be crossed off your list of suspects pretty quickly."

"Whoever said she was on it?"

"Well… I just overheard, you know, someone suggesting it."

"Maybe you shouldn't listen to gossip."

"So does that mean she's in the clear?"

"That's something only time will tell." Tate smiled tightly and leaned forward, shifting his weight to stand. Pushing his hand into his jeans pocket, he retrieved a business card and slid it across the table towards me. "That's my number. If you think of anything else, please reach out. Now if you'll excuse me, I have work to do. Thanks for your time, Aubrey." He took a step away from me.

"Oh, hang on a second!" I hurriedly stood and moved behind him. "I have your jacket. It's up in my room though. Do you want to wait while I get it?"

"No, I'll follow you. I want to double-check something in Willow's room anyway. After you." His arm stretched out, suggesting I lead the way.

I felt all eyes on me as we crossed the room. Ellie gave me the thumbs-up as Nancy's lips puckered disapprovingly, and Beverley stared longingly at Tate. Not that I could blame her. He was a pretty good sight first thing in the morning, and despite his veiled warning that I stay out of the investigation, I had enjoyed sharing my coffee with him.

CHAPTER FIVE

"Was that the Detective I saw exiting your bedroom?" Spencer dropped a bowl of cereal onto the table and pulled a chair opposite me as I tucked into the bacon and egg muffin I'd been drooling over.

"Yeah. I was giving him back his jacket."

"Huh." He sat heavily.

"Why?"

"No reason. Just thought it was early for the good detective to be working."

"I had breakfast with him."

Spencer's jaw ticked. Picking up his spoon he shoveled muesli into his mouth, his eyes broody.

"He had more questions about Willow's death," I explained. "He might be looking for you, actually."

"Why me?"

"Because I told him about Ricky and how you were speaking to him. I think he wants to know more about why Ricky was here when he wasn't on the guest list."

"As if I know," Spencer mumbled between mouthfuls.

I took a moment to study him. "Are you okay? You seem a bit uptight."

"I missed my morning run."

"How come?"

"As I was leaving for it, I spotted Chris heading up the stairs to Willow's room."

"Geez, considering it's a no-go zone, it seems to have more visitors than Macy's during a sale."

"Exactly why I was intrigued. The room is taped off, so he has no reason to be there. And after what you said last night about someone being up there, it made me curious about what he could be doing."

"Ah, so you are interested in investigating this." I smiled.

"Look, I don't know Jenna as well as you both do, but I do believe she's innocent, and I'd hate to think Tate could pin this on her."

"I'm sure he'll figure out the truth. He looks pretty good at his job."

Spencer frowned. "Does he? If he's so good, then he wouldn't be suspecting Jenna in the first place."

Fair point.

"Back to Chris," I interrupted. "What was he doing in Willow's room? Did you follow him to see what he was up to?"

"Kind of. I knew I couldn't go up there, as he would be suspicious of why, so I hung around on the first-floor landing."

"And?"

"He never came back down. I waited a good twenty minutes, but when only silence drifted down toward me, I tiptoed up for a look." He took a spoonful of muesli and crunched loudly.

"What did you see?"

"Nothing," Spencer mumbled around his breakfast.

I stared at him open-mouthed, willing him to hurry up, so I could hear the rest of what he had to say. Swallowing hard, he picked up his cup and sipped his coffee.

"Spencer, I'm aging here. Can you please finish your story before I get gray hair?"

His eyes darted to my head, and mischief crinkled the corners of his eyes. "Is that…?"

My hand shot to my hair as I gasped. "No! It is not! It's highlights."

"If you say so," he teased.

"Can we please get back to Chris?" I huffed. "What did you see when you reached the top of the stairs?"

"I told you. Nothing. Police tape crossed Willow's closed door, so I listened at it instead. When I heard silence, I quietly opened it a crack to look inside."

I leaned in, my eyes locked on to him, holding my breath.

"Only the room was empty," Spencer finished.

"Where did Chris go?"

"How would I know?"

"It's part of your job to be curious about these things."

"I'm far better leaving that to my imagination." Spencer wiggled his eyebrows suggestively, and my heart skipped a beat. But then maybe that was the coffee kicking in.

"Hmmm, so that's two people in Willow's room who disappeared without coming back down the stairs."

Spencer nodded.

"How does that even happen? I guess it's possible Chris abseiled out the window, but last night I definitely heard footsteps heading down."

Spencer rolled his eyes. "Abseiling? I can see why you're such a good fiction writer."

A warm glow burned behind my chest bone despite the inkling that may not have been a compliment.

"This house is pretty old," I commented, picking up my cup. "Maybe it's holding a secret that we haven't uncovered yet."

"Like?"

I shrugged. It was way too early to figure out that conundrum.

"I forgot to tell Tate how I saw Chris on the stairs right before finding Willow." I put my cup down and slapped my hand against my forehead. "And I never did get his phone number."

"Sharing phone numbers already?" Spencer probed, his grin not quite making it to his eyes.

"He wants to be the first to know if I remember anything else."

"Huh."

Before I could question his indifference, Ellie bounded toward us. "Hey guys, did you hear that Isla has called us all into the library? She wants to address what's going to happen around the retreat."

"Right now?"

"Uh-huh. Come on. I've saved seats for you both."

I left Spencer to finish his breakfast and made a quick stop in the ladies' bathroom. Ellie went ahead to prevent Nancy from stealing our prized seats at the back of the room, closest to the door. I always liked that position for several reasons. One was we were the first to exit and make our way to the dining room, but it also had the added advantage of there being very little chance of being called for audience participation.

As I rounded the corner, loud voices traveled toward me from behind a closed door. The shiny brass plaque told me the room was the manager's, and the voices told me that Chris was having a disagreement.

"What you did was bad enough," a female voice screamed. "Don't try to turn this on me."

"Stop!" Chris yelled. "You got what you wanted so leave it alone."

Silence took a beat.

"Are you serious? I never got anywhere near what I wanted, and you know it. You never kept up your end of the agreement."

"It wasn't an agreement!"

Voices lowered, and I checked that the hallway was empty before moving closer to the door, intrigued.

"Okay," she continued. "Whatever you want to call it. The facts are either pay up, or I tell Isla what you did."

Chris's sigh was loud. "Listen. I'm sick of this. I talked Willow into not firing you. Wasn't that enough? Now you're here with even more threats."

Was Chris with Naomi?

Pushing my ear against the wood door, I closed my eyes and concentrated my hearing, wanting to know what he'd done and what she was demanding.

Naomi laughed. "What you did yesterday changed everything. So tell me, how much is it worth to keep Isla from learning the truth about what you did to her sister?"

I gasped. Did Chris kill Willow? How did Naomi know about it? Was that what she'd been talking about on the phone last night? Or was she involved in Willow's death too?

My heart raced with possibilities.

"Aubrey! What are you doing?"

I squelched a scream as I nearly jumped out of my skin and spun to see Spencer frowning down at me.

"Geez Louise! You scared the bejesus out of me," I complained, clutching my chest and wondering if twenty-eight was too young for a heart attack.

"If you weren't so busy eavesdropping, maybe you would've heard me walk up behind you."

I grabbed his arm and pulled him away from the door, hoping that Chris and Naomi hadn't heard us.

"I wasn't eavesdropping. I was… okay, I was eavesdropping," I whispered. "But you couldn't have picked a worse time to creep up on me."

Spencer looked confused.

"I think Chris killed Willow." I threw a side-eyed glare his way as the door to the manager's office burst open, and Chris stepped outside, his skin blotchy. His gaze fell to us, and his lips tightened as his eyes narrowed.

"Oh, hi, Chris," I cooed, widening my eyes and hoping I looked innocent.

"What are you doing?" he snapped, his gaze flipping between the two of us.

"Just heading to the little girls' room when I bumped into Spencer, and he startled me." I brightened my smile, tapping Spencer's chest, nudging him to go along with me.

Oh boy, there were a few muscles under that shirt. Heat flushed my face, and I wasn't sure if I wanted Chris to think I was hot for Spencer's chest or for Spencer to think I was guilty of eavesdropping on Chris. Either way wasn't great for me.

Thankfully, Isla stepped along the corridor, a vertical line deep between her brows.

"Everything okay?" she asked, her gaze flipping between us all.

Chris cleared his throat and pulled the door closed behind him, blocking our view to the inside.

"Yes. I was just finishing up some business when I heard a commotion in the hall." His gaze pinned me to the spot.

Spencer stepped up. "No commotion. I just bumped into Aubrey and scared her. Everyone's on edge after what happened yesterday."

I hurriedly checked Chris's reaction, but his stony gaze was locked onto Isla.

"Yes, well that's what I need to speak to everyone about." Her jaw flexed as she asked, "Did you get the message about the meeting in the library?"

I nodded.

"Good. We start in five minutes."

As she turned away, I saw the tears brimming her lashes, and my heart went out to her.

"Isla," I called after her. "I just wanted to say how sorry I am about Willow. I understand what you're feeling."

She stopped abruptly as she faced me. "Thank you for your kindness, but I'm not sure how you could." She blinked back the tears, and a fierceness replaced her vulnerability.

"I lost my sister a year ago. I know the ache left in my heart after losing her." The familiar pain that I'd pushed down reared inside me and caused my eyes to sting. But I'd learned how to move past it. Not to dishonor my sister's memory, but because if I didn't, I'd crack into a million pieces, and I had no idea how I would put myself back together.

"I'm sorry to hear that, Aubrey. I really am. But it's not quite the same, is it? Did the police think your sister was murdered?" Her arched brows disappeared under her bangs.

"Umm, no. They didn't. I never had any answers as to what really happened other than they thought she fell asleep driving. That never sat well with me as Emily thrived on only a few hours of sleep a night. She was like the Energizer bunny on steroids—but without the drugs," I hurriedly added. "I've had to make peace with the fact that I'll never know what made her leave the road and hit the tree that night. As awful as it is having the police asking so many questions, I hope they can give you the answers you need."

Isla swallowed hard. "Thank you. I appreciate your thoughts, and I'm sorry you had to experience something so horrible." Compassion welled behind her lashes, but she quickly blinked it away. "Now if you'll excuse me, I'll see you in the library."

Isla may be more like Willow than I thought.

As her steps hurried her away, Spencer moved in close behind me. "I didn't know that about your sister." His voice was low and filled with sympathy. I knew the tone well, and I hated it. I'd heard it many times over the past year, and as much as I knew that whoever was saying the words meant them, it was always followed by an uncomfortable silence, whereby both of us wanted to run. This time was no different.

"It's not something I usually talk about." Looking over my shoulder, I gave Spencer a smile that told him it was okay. He didn't need to make me feel better or to say those empty words, *if there's anything I can do*. Of course, he would mean them, but what could he do? He couldn't bring back the dead, and nothing but that would relieve any of the pain I felt when I thought of her.

Apparently only time would do that, but until that moment, pushing it all down inside me was the best way forward. At least in public. In the middle of the night when there was nothing but memories, the tears could flow, and my heart could break. But no one wanted to see that.

I pulled my shoulders back and turned swiftly. Then came face-to-face with Chris.

"What were you really doing standing there?" he demanded.

"I wasn't doing anything," I lied, swallowing hard. "I told you I was on my way to the bathroom when I bumped into Spencer. I'm really jumpy after what happened to Willow."

I studied Chris for a reaction, but he held the facade.

"It's amazing how Isla's holding up," I pushed.

"Yes, she's a strong woman. But she has me to help get her through this difficult time."

Other than Ellie, I'd had no one except my parents and brother to help me through, but their own grief had been too heavy for me to have placed any more on their shoulders. I hoped that Isla had better support than a murderous husband to get her through it.

"That's good. She'll need you."

"Hey, Chris," Spencer cut in. "Someone was in Willow's room. Around one a.m. Then you were in there later this morning. Isn't it taped off by the police?"

Chris stiffened. "I have no idea who has been in there, but it sure as hell wasn't me." His tone was smooth, yet his fingers clenched into a fist. "Why would I go into a crime scene? That's insane."

"You were in there about an hour ago, though?"

A muscle twitched in Chris's jaw, his smile just a little too tight. "No. Wasn't me. But you shouldn't be concerning yourself with things like that. Why don't you stick to writing and leave the questions for the police? After all, they're the professionals." His voice was light, but as he shifted his weight, my stomach twisted.

Spencer frowned. "Aubrey, didn't you say you saw Chris on the stairs just before you found Willow?"

I nodded.

"What of it?" Chris challenged. "I manage this place. I'm often on the stairs. Only I was nowhere near that room." A muscle ticked near his eye as he cleared his throat. "But it's possible someone from housekeeping was."

"Surely they weren't granted access."

"No. No, they weren't. I should go and have a word with them. Thank you for alerting me to it. Now if you'll excuse me, I have a lot to do." He double-checked the door had closed behind him then strode away, purpose making his steps rapid.

Unease gnawed at my stomach.

"He's hiding something," Spencer mused. "But what?"

"I need to tell you what I overheard," I whispered, knowing Naomi was still in Chris's office and may very well be listening at the door. "But not here. Not now."

"Sure, we'll go to the library and find out what's happening. We can chat about Chris later."

"Alrighty, but I really do need to visit the little girls' room first."

Spencer grinned. "Don't be long. We don't want Isla any more upset than she already is."

Once Spencer made his way to the library, I answered the call of nature and then went to follow him. Only as I passed Chris's office, I spotted Naomi hurrying along the hall.

Curiosity prickled my skin as my gaze fell to the door, and I wondered what secrets it held. It definitely sounded like Naomi was blackmailing Chris over Willow's death. But why had he been in Willow's room that morning? Was it to remove something that would link him to the murder? Could the evidence now be in his office?

Writing murder mysteries gave me the insight that to murder someone you had to have means, motive, and opportunity. Pushing someone out of a window definitely gave him the means. Chris had the opportunity, as I saw him coming down the stairs right after she would have been murdered. But what was his motive?

Taking a fast look around me to ensure I was alone, I tentatively reached out and turned the knob to his office door. The lock clicked, and the door snapped open an inch. My breath caught as I reconsidered snooping. But I'd be quick. And it would just be a fast scan of the room to see if anything would give me an idea of why he would have killed Willow.

Without stopping to second guess myself, my blood pounded in my ears as I pushed the door open and slithered into the room.

Quietly closing it behind me, I took a moment to lean back and slow my breathing. I felt dizzy as adrenalin caused my pulse to surge. But I didn't want to be longer than necessary, so I tightened my pelvic floor muscles and blinked rapidly as I scanned the room.

Nothing exceptional about it really. The same dark hardwood flooring that was throughout the home. Mahogany bookcases lined one wall, their shelves filled with dark leather spines. An Apple MacBook sat on a sparse desk, a black office chair tucked neatly under it. Several photos sat on the polished surface, Post-it notes stuck to the frames. I scurried toward them, hoping to learn more about Chris.

One of the photos was of Isla, a dreamy look in her eyes as she gazed at him, his arm draped lovingly over her shoulder. They looked like the perfect couple and a twinge of envy stabbed at my heart. Until I recalled that he could be a murderer.

The next photo was a group photo of him standing behind Willow as Isla linked arms with her and a woman who I thought could be their mother. The family resemblance was strong.

Moving my attention from the photos, I sank into the leather desk chair and lifted the lid on the laptop. My hand shook as I clicked the trackpad, the screen flashing to life. I wondered what Chris's password might be.

I typed in Isla's name but got nothing. Hmmm, did he have a dog? I hurriedly typed a few common dog names but came up dry. I typed in his own name, even trying a combination of characters to replace letters, but still nothing. Looking around the room for clues, my gaze fell to a copy of Willow's latest book before I glanced back at the family photo. Intuition buzzed loud in my ears as my fingers moved rapidly over the keyboard, and I typed *W- I- L- L- O- W*.

My heart pounded as the screen sprang to life, and I had full access to Chris's files.

Well, that was interesting.

My fingers fumbled as I clicked on a few desktop icons but found nothing more than correspondence from clients, a few employee documents, and a to-do list as long as my arm, giving me a whole new respect for anyone that ran a B&B. Locating the email icon, I clicked, hoping to find something incriminating. I really had no idea what I was doing other than following the steps I put my heroines through.

Chris was nothing if not tidy. He had no stray documents or photos haphazardly messing up his laptop. Everything was neatly located in folders within folders, and as I hurriedly scrolled over them, nothing jumped out at me. Until I stopped on an email from Willow dated two months ago.

It's our secret, but I think this will be my next bestseller.

I clicked on the attachment titled *The Black Rose* and gasped. Oh wowzers! That was Willow's latest novel.

A thrill jumped in my belly that I was so close to her latest work, and I couldn't fight the urge to start reading.

Three sentences in, and I understood why she was a *New York Times* best-selling author, and I had every confidence that her hunch about this manuscript had been correct. I was already hooked. My eyes skimmed the words at lightning speeds, and I hurriedly scrolled through the pages, wanting to take in as many words as I could. Only I knew that I had to finish searching Chris's files and get out of there as quickly as possible. But her words seduced me, pulling me into a world that I didn't want to leave. *Urgh!* Jenna was right. This book was going to be amazing. I could already see why Heron and Heron had signed her.

I was just getting lost in the hero's embrace when Chris's voice boomed outside of the door, causing me to jolt. It also appeared that in the fight, flight, or freeze scenario, freeze was the reaction my body had as my fingers stopped on the trackpad, and my eyes were locked on the door.

The handle turned, and my heart missed a beat. Thankfully, my freeze instinct moved to flight, and I slammed the laptop shut, my gaze leaving the door and searching for a place to hide.

But where? Under the desk? No way. That was far too dangerous.

Behind the curtains? Maybe, but how long could I stay there without being noticed?

My gaze stopped on the window. Was it locked? I sure hoped not.

Chris' voice rang through the closed door as he called to the housekeeper to give Nancy some fresh towels, and I said a silent prayer to the universe to give me the moment I needed.

Rushing toward the window, I fumbled with the catch as the door handle slowly turned.

My blood pressure moved into the stratosphere, and a cry strangled in my throat as I searched for a viable excuse to be found opening his window.

Thankfully, the gods were on my side today, as the housekeeper's voice mingled with Chris's, and the doorknob was released. I gave a shaky breath and thanked the universe as Chris stopped to chat. I took a deep breath, eased the window open, and launched myself outside, pushing the pane closed behind me.

* * *

The library had an intimate feel with the plush carpeting, wall-to-wall bookshelves filled with the classics, and worn leather armchairs waiting to be sat in. The crystal chandelier hung heavy from the ornate plastered ceiling, table lamps filled the room with a warm glow, and the faint scent of beeswax on the polished shelves instantly calmed me.

At the front of the room Kara's dark eyes sparkled with mischief as she fiddled with the ends of her long black hair. She was deep in conversation with Beverley, whose cheeks were glowing. I didn't need two guesses to know what they were talking about.

Isla stood near the window, her back to us, her phone to her ear, her words quiet and inaudible.

As my knees shook and my legs threatened to give out on me, I ignored them all and slid into a chair between Ellie and Spencer

"Everything okay?" Ellie asked, her gaze darting toward me. "You took an awful long time in the bathroom. I wondered if the stress was getting to your stomach."

Spencer suppressed a small smile, and heat ran up my neck and into my cheeks. I hit Ellie with a glare.

"Nah. I'm fine, but thanks for that visual." I lowered my voice and moved my lips close to her ear, nodding for Spencer to lean in.

"You look like you lost a fight with a shrub," he commented, gently removing a twig from my hair.

I swallowed hard. "I jumped out of the window in Chris's office."

"What!" Ellie's eyes widened.

"*Shhh*," I warned.

"Sorry. What were you doing?" she whispered.

"Well, you told us to investigate." I hurriedly filled them in on the Naomi-Chris scenario. "Considering I think he could be the murderer, I figured it couldn't hurt to have a look around."

Spencer groaned as Ellie spun in her seat to glare at me. "You should have at least had a lookout. Next time make sure you don't do it alone."

Next time? My heart had nearly exploded the first time. I had a whole new sympathy for the heroines I wrote about.

"What did you find?" Ellie's eyes were large and round.

Isla still had her back to us as her fingernail slowly picked at a leather-bound book, so I checked that no one was within listening distance and pressed on.

"Willow's name is the password to his laptop, and he had a photo of her on his desk. I don't have a photo of my brother-in-law on my desk. Don't you think that's odd?"

"You don't have a brother-in-law," Ellie reminded me.

"Okay, my sister-in-law then."

"I'm sure Chris loved her in a very unique way."

"By unique you mean weird, right?"

"No. I mean, they're family. I have heaps of photos of my family on my desk."

"But her name was his password! That's super weird."

"True." Ellie nodded.

"Maybe Chris is the stalker Tate was questioning me about." My thoughts danced over possibilities.

"Nah. He's too good-looking for that."

"What? Can't good-looking men be weirdos?" This was news to me.

"No. It's more like he could have whoever he wanted. He wouldn't have to stalk someone."

"Let's not forget that tiny detail—he's married," Spencer added sarcastically.

I was going to say more only my attention was grabbed by Nancy as she entered the room, closely followed by Jenna. Jenna gave us a small smile as she made her way toward Isla, and my heart cracked just a little bit for her. She looked broken. Her face was pale, dark circles heavy beneath her lower lashes. Her arms crossed her body as she hugged her iPad close to her, and her shoulders drooped.

Isla noticed her and ended the call. As she cast a quick look around the room, she cleared her throat to address our group while Nancy slid into a chair alongside Beverley.

"Looks like you're all here. Thank you for coming. It's been a very stressful twelve hours, and I'm sure you all want to go home. I apologize for the inconvenience this has caused you, but please be assured we are still committed to this retreat. We are, however, prepared to offer a partial refund to you for the time you've missed this weekend, and I wanted to let you know Jenna has agreed to complete the retreat on behalf of Willow if you'd prefer to stay."

I recoiled, shocked by her words. I looked at Jenna as she gave a weak smile, and I guessed it hadn't really been her choice.

"Thanks, Isla," Jenna continued quietly. "I have all of Willow's notes here." She tapped the cover of her iPad. "So, I feel confident that I can give the presentations she had for you. Of course, the one-on-one sessions won't happen…" Her voice broke before she took a slow breath. "Isla has kindly agreed to refund that portion of the retreat for those of you who wish to continue on."

"I understand that circumstances are difficult," Isla interrupted. "But it's what Willow would have wanted. Now, I'll give you some time to think about it. Snacks will be served in the dining room at ten-thirty, and Jenna will give the first presentation after lunch. For those who want to go home, please let me know. I wish you all the best with your writing endeavors." She nodded toward the room as low murmurs broke out. "Now, please excuse me. I have duties that I need to attend to."

She held her head high as she strutted from the room, but the tremble of her bottom lip as she passed us told the truth about what was going on inside her.

Once she had exited the room, Ellie turned to me. "Oh my goodness, can you believe they want to keep the retreat going?"

"I'm betting Jenna wasn't really on board with that decision," I agreed.

"Let's ask her." Ellie leaped from her seat and pushed past Beverley as she made her way toward Jenna.

By the time I caught up with her, Jenna was halfway through a sentence.

"…why don't we meet for lunch," Jenna said to Ellie, her smile hiding the true meaning of her words, her eyes darting to the small queue forming behind her.

I grabbed Ellie's arm before she could argue. "Come on. Jenna has a job to do. We can talk to her later."

Ellie glared at Beverley, but I think she got the message that now was not the time Jenna was going to divulge any truths, so we would have to wait until we could sit quietly with her.

Spencer joined us as I led the way to the dining room, hoping to find a spot where we could talk without being overheard.

The dining room was positioned at the back of the house, the view from the floor-to-ceiling windows breathtaking as it looked over the lake. Outside the sky was gray, the wind howled, and snow was only days away. Thankfully, the roaring fireplace kept the cold at bay.

Six highly polished mahogany dining tables were scattered around the large room, made to feel cozy with the deep red paneled walls, wide window casings, and intricately patterned crown molding. Large mirrors reflected the view, and a sideboard held an always hot water urn and an assortment of tea and coffee cups to keep the guests hydrated. At the moment, we were the only ones there, so I bypassed it all and pulled out a chair at a table in front of the window.

"I bet Isla pressured Jenna into doing this stupid retreat," Ellie spat, sitting heavily alongside me. Spencer sat opposite her, his gaze lost toward the lake. "Jenna needs to be home, snuggling her cat and practicing self-care, not here following directions that Willow has left. I mean who even thinks to do such a thing?" Ellie threw her hands in the air.

"I guess Isla felt compelled to finish what Willow started," I added despite agreeing with Ellie and wondering what Isla's true intentions were.

"Well, we're not staying and putting that pressure on our friend," Ellie stated.

"Of course not! But…" I bit my lip.

"What? But what?"

"Well, I'm going to guess from the keen look in Beverley's eye as she rushed Jenna, that she at least will want to finish the weekend. And wouldn't it be better if we stayed and supported her? Of course, I'm not interested in the presentations," I quickly added. "But why don't we see how many people, if any, want to continue? I'd hate to leave Jenna alone."

Ellie held her breath for a second as she considered me. She then turned to Spencer. "What about you, Spence? What are you going to do?"

"Are you both staying?" he asked, turning his attention to me before lifting his laptop from his bag and placing it on the table.

Ellie and I nodded.

"Then count me in. Quality time with you both is always on top of my to-do list. Right up with not letting you get murdered. But for now, I've got to put some words on the page before my editor hunts *me* down."

* * *

I liked Spencer's thinking. Jenna seemed tied up, and until she was ready to talk to us, I figured I may as well get some work done. Ellie said she needed some air and had left us alone, so copying Spencer, I opened my bag and retrieved my laptop. I wasn't sure how much I would get done as Spencer's musky aftershave could be pretty distracting, but I was determined to do my best. Thankfully, the words began to flow.

The inside of Bernie's house was just the way I remembered it. The shiplap walls were painted white, the windows were floor-to-ceiling glass showcasing the amazing aqua blue ocean, the floors were well-loved wide teak planks, and the mostly white painted furniture was eclectic. One wall held a bookcase bursting with dog-eared books, a handful of family photos, and a bevy of colorful crystals. I picked up a pink orb and rubbed the smooth surface as I gazed at the pictures.

My mom was an only child, and I was her only child, so our family wasn't large. But it had been filled to the brim with love, which now radiated out at me from the smiles of those I cherished. Including Bernie. Her wrinkled face showed her years of surfing and loving the sun, wispy gray hairs escaped her long braids, and dangly silver earrings adorned her ears. Four necklaces, each with green stones, hung low on her chest, and her vibrancy for life shone from her blue eyes.

She was beautiful, loving, and adored by everyone around her. When news traveled that she'd passed away after a bad fall down the stairs resulting in a broken neck, the entire town was devastated.

"Can you please recap the events leading to the discovery?" A middle-aged detective in a wool suit frowned across at me. Perspiration dripped from his temple, and he used a cloth handkerchief to dab it away, his suffering evident in his expression.

"Are you sure I can't offer you a glass of water?" To be honest, I was worried he might have heat stroke.

Detective Henry Gilbraith looked very out of place in the small beach shack. In fact, he looked like he'd made a wrong turn at the airport and hadn't realized it yet. His gaze roamed the room with disbelief mixed with confusion, yet his large gray eyes were sharp, briefly stopping on every little detail. His skin was pale, his hair was thin, and his shoes were polished. Well, they were before he'd trudged through the sand.

"I'm fine, thank you." He dismissed my concern with a wave of his hand. "Don't mind me. This is my first day in Saltwater Bay, and I underestimated the humidity. If you'll excuse me, I might just slip off my jacket." He didn't wait for my reply. Instead, he placed his notebook on the large upturned woven fisherman's basket that acted as a coffee table and unbuttoned his jacket. Once he'd removed it, he carefully folded it in half and laid it over the back of the white linen couch.

"Now, where were we?" he asked, loosening his striped tie. "Oh yes. The skull found under the house. Tell me again how you found it."

I smiled. Despite his stuffy appearance, I quite liked the detective already.

"It's my first day here too." I placed the orb back on the shelf and moved to sit on the couch opposite him. "Well, it's my first day back in town. Growing up, this was like a second home to me."

The detective nodded as he regarded the mound of cushions on the chair behind him. Indecision filled the deep crevice in between his brows before he gently moved one aside and perched on the edge of the seat.

"Saltwater Bay is quite... different from what I'm used to," he said. "Much hotter."

"What are you used to?"

"Being the one to ask the questions." His smile was kind yet told me he was in charge. "Now, recap how you found the skull."

I gulped as Keagan Murphy smirked behind him. Once I'd recounted everything from when I'd dropped my suitcase in the sand to Grayson showing me the skull, I sank back into the soft cushions and rubbed my face. How did my return start so badly?

I smiled to myself, happy with the foundation I'd laid for the goal and motivation for Daphne's actions, and the conflict she was about to face. I knew what she wanted to do, why she wanted to do it, and who was going to stop her. For me, getting all that believable was often the hardest part of the writing process. Fleshing it out and learning who my characters were going to be was the exciting part. And despite loving Stoney Creek, when winter hit hard, I was often guilty of dreaming of somewhere in the tropics. It didn't matter where in the world it was so long as it was hot. Next to my characters, it was the thing I loved the most about writing. I could travel anywhere within seconds of opening the page, and Saltwater Bay was going to be a fun place to visit.

I looked up from my words as Jenna's voice floated across the dining room toward me, breaking me from my imaginary world.

"I could hardly say no." She waved her protest as Ellie stomped alongside her. "Isla said it's what Willow would have wanted, and I'd already done all the work making the slides. It's not much for me to stand up there and give the presentation." Stopping at our table, her eyes closed momentarily as she took a shallow breath, defeat oozing from her every pore. "Besides, Isla said I'd get paid if I did it."

Ellie's shoulders dropped as she pulled to a halt. "But why did Beverley want to continue?"

Jenna shrugged. "She said she was going to spend the rest of the weekend here, and as I was willing to impart the information, she couldn't see a reason not to take the offer up. And Kara backed her up, so what could I say?"

"At least you're not Detective Tate's number one suspect anymore." I closed the lid on my laptop as I looked up at them.

Ellie's neck lengthened as she pulled out the closest chair and sat heavily. "You never told us this."

"Well, I don't know for certain, but when I told him about Ricky and how he killed off his last character, Tate seemed very interested to follow it up."

"Spence, have you seen Ricky?" Ellie asked. "Did you learn anymore about why Willow was going to fire Naomi?"

He shook his head, blinking himself from his work. "I haven't learned anything new, but I did see Jonathan Berkley when I got my bag back out of the car and rechecked into my room."

Ellie gasped, her eyes brightening. "Where did you see him? Do you think he'll be joining us at dinner tonight? I know these aren't the best circumstances, but I'd love to meet him."

"He was coming out of the room opposite mine."

"How did he look?" I asked.

"Sad."

"Like sad as in the-love-of-my-life-just-died, or sad as in I-just-killed-the-love-of-my-life?" Ellie probed.

"Hang on a second." Jenna put her hand up to halt us, simultaneously sitting alongside me. "Berkley's asked for privacy so neither of you annoy him. Please. But why would you think he killed Willow?"

I, too, was curious about this, especially as I thought we already had Chris pinned as the murderer.

"Because my theory is maybe he found out that Willow and Levi had started up a relationship again."

"Ellie, you can't say that," I interrupted. "I clearly saw Willow telling Levi to stay away from her. We have no reason to think that Jonathan Berkley had a reason to kill her. He loved her."

"Weeeelllll…" Jenna bit her lip, garnering our complete attention.

"Oh my goodness!" Ellie squealed, leaning her elbows on the table. "You know something. Come on then. Spill the beans."

"I don't know for sure," Jenna warned. "But I think Willow and Berkley were a thing of the past."

"You've kept gossip like this from us?" Ellie looked hurt.

"You know how I feel about gossip. It's the work of the devil."

"Was it gossip or was it real?" I asked, agreeing with Jenna in principle but also wanting to know all the sordid details.

Jenna bit her lip. "Willow never told me for sure, but I overheard a phone conversation with her yesterday morning begging Berkley to reconsider. She said she was sorry for what she'd done and was going to make it right."

"Make what right?" I probed.

"I don't know, but I'm sure it's why he pulled out of the weekend retreat at the last minute. I didn't know he was even here until Chris told me he'd checked in."

"He arrived yesterday," Ellie added. "Right before Willow was killed."

Spencer rolled his eyes as Ellie got caught up in the drama of the situation.

Jenna smiled and placed a hand on Ellie's arm. "I love that you're thinking outside the box, but I really don't think Berkley would kill her. Even if the relationship was over."

Ellie screwed her lips together before opening the notes section in her cell phone and tapping away.

"Jenna, is there any reason Chris would have Willow's latest manuscript?" I asked.

Jenna narrowed her eyes as she considered me. "Why would you ask that?"

"Ummm…" Ellie and Spencer both knew I'd been snooping, but did I want to make Jenna an accessory to my mini B&E? "I overheard him talking to someone about it, and I wondered if they had some kind of business connections." I crossed my fingers, hoping to negate my partial lie.

Jenna shrugged. "Not that I know of, but maybe she'd ask him to read over it before she submitted it to Heron and Heron."

"Like was he an editor? Beta reader?"

"No idea. Willow could be private at times and often didn't share with me, though."

I guessed that could explain the secrecy in the email telling Chris that no one could know about the manuscript but them.

"Jenna, did Ricky leave after the break yesterday?" Spencer asked.

She shrugged. "I called him an Uber, but I didn't wait for it to arrive."

"So, you didn't actually see him leave?"

"No. I had a few last-minute calls to make. I left him at the front entrance and made my way to the library. Why?"

"Just placing everyone at the time of the murder." Spencer looked over Ellie's shoulder as she tapped away at her notes.

Jenna sighed as she checked her watch. "Are you all going to come to the afternoon session?"

"No. We've all agreed you shouldn't be working, and us being there will only put pressure on you," I stated.

"It really won't. In fact, I think I'd feel better if you were there." Jenna leaned forward, her eyes wide as she gazed at each of us. "I'm not going to lie. I really just want to go home, but Isla promised me that I would get paid my share of the retreat proceeds if she doesn't have to issue refunds. So, I don't have much choice. It'll be enough to keep the bank happy for a week or so."

"What's this afternoon's session about?" Spencer asked.

"Estate planning for authors."

"Boring," Ellie whispered.

"Yeah, but it's important to be prepared. Look what's happened to Willow. She never expected that."

"Do you think Isla's the beneficiary of Willow's will?" Spencer asked.

We all shrugged.

"I would imagine so," replied Jenna. "She's her next of kin."

"That's interesting," Ellie added.

"Not really. It's what I would expect," Jenna added.

"Yeah, but don't they say to follow the money?" Spencer questioned.

"True, but not Isla. She had nothing but gratitude and love for Willow."

My neck lengthened as pieces clicked together in my head. "Maybe, but as Chris is Isla's husband then he'd benefit from that money too."

That was a motive if ever I'd heard one.

CHAPTER SIX

It was midafternoon by the time that Jenna finished her presentation on wills, and as much as I hated to admit it, I needed to get one written. I didn't own a lot in this world other than a mortgaged houseboat that was moored on the lake, but in the event of my death, my tiny parrot Axel needed to have a home.

I flipped a page in my notebook and made a list of who I wanted to give what. My brother, Corey, would get my car, not that he'd be excited about owning an old red Honda Civic. Even if it was the two-door model and, in my honest opinion, was fantastic. I would give Ellie my powder pink Prada tote. It had taken me years to save for it and was the only extravagant thing I owned, but I knew she coveted it, and it would look fantastic on her arm. Mom and Dad would get the little part of my home that I owned and any future royalties that I got from my books. Hmmm, what else did I have of any value?

Drumming my pen between my teeth, I looked down at the page and frowned. It was quite sad really, laying everything you held dear out on paper and realizing how little you owned. Before doing this exercise, I'd been quite happy with where I was in life, but this only highlighted how unsuccessful I was.

I dropped the pen on the desk as I sat back and sighed. Ellie and Spencer were writing furiously, Beverley and Nancy were sitting in front of me, both carefully writing lists, and Kara looked bored. I took a moment to study them all. Could any of them have been Willow's killer? Hmmm, we'd never actually considered that. But what reason would any of them have to harm her?

To be honest, I didn't know much about any of them other than what we had learned when we'd introduced ourselves at the beginning of the retreat. Kara was from Bellingham, Beverley was from Boise, and Nancy was from Miles City, Montana. So, what reason would any of them have for killing Willow? And besides, Willow held the key to their careers. If they could get her to give a review for the cover of their latest novel, it would be an instant best seller. No, it was in all our interests for Willow to be safe and well.

I flipped my notebook closed, doodled on the cover, and allowed my mind to wander. I was pretty tired and was struggling to keep my thoughts on track, and it didn't take long before I was aimlessly considering the number of notebooks I owned and how I really needed to check that new stationery store in town for some new ones.

Ellie sighed loudly and ripped the page she was working on out of her book. Only the tear wasn't as effective as I was sure she'd meant it to be, as it took two goes for her to remove it. Thumping it onto the table alongside her, she started to scribble furiously on a clean page.

I looked at the torn paper she'd discarded, and my mind jumped to the note that I'd found in the garden the night before and remembered, other than a curious first glance, I never had given it much attention. At the time, the page had been too wet to work out the handwriting, and I'd been waiting for it to dry.

But now I wondered where it had come from. And how had it ended up in the mulch?

I sat up straight as a tendril of a thought snaked into my mind. What if Willow had been holding it when she fell? If so, how had the police missed it? Or maybe they hadn't missed it. Maybe they saw it and had thought it was just a scrap piece of paper blown in on the wind. So why was it bothering me now?

Leaning toward Ellie, I tapped her arm. She immediately stopped scribbling and lifted her gaze to me.

"Hey, I'm going back to my room for a while. There's something I need to take a closer look at."

"What are you talking about?"

I hurriedly explained my late-night garden adventure.

"Aubrey, it could have belonged to anyone."

"I know, which is why I'm going to have a closer look at it. I took a photo of the notes Willow had written on the whiteboard yesterday, so I have a sample of her handwriting. I want to see if it matches what's on the paper."

"Do you think it was a suicide note or something like that?"

Now there was a thought that hadn't occurred to me.

"Why haven't we considered that before?" I asked, my mind whirling at a thousand miles an hour.

"Because of the marks on her neck," Spencer added, eavesdropping into the conversation.

"We never asked if they could have been made earlier, though."

Ellie shook her head. "No. We would have seen them when she was doing her presentation."

"That's true." I bit my lip. "Then maybe the note was from someone demanding something from her, and she didn't want to pay." My imagination was running into overdrive.

"Like a blackmail letter?" Ellie's eyes widened.

My thoughts flipped to Naomi and Chris. Naomi did make the comment about Chris doing something to Willow and Isla finding out. I gasped.

"We need to find out." I pushed my books into my bag and stood, throwing the strap over my shoulder.

Ellie shrugged but closed her notes and stood. "Spence, are you coming?"

"Sure. I'm going cross-eyed here, so a distraction might save me from accidentally leaving my Def Leppard collection to Gran. She still thinks 'Pour Some Sugar on Me' is about baking." He lifted a shoulder.

"You have a Def Leppard collection?" Ellie asked.

"Sure do. They're classics." He copied Ellie, packing everything into his backpack, and stood. As he stared down at me, my thoughts were racing over Chris and Willow arguing and him trying to strangle her and pushing her out the window. Okay, my imagination was running wild. Reining it in, I hurriedly followed after Ellie and Spence.

As we all exited the room and made our way upstairs, Spencer said, "Tell me again why you think this page is connected to Willow."

"I don't know for sure that it is, but why did the universe put it in my path?"

"Because you're clumsy as heck, and the universe never misses an opportunity to mess with you." Spencer chuckled.

"I think Willow was speaking to you from the other side," Ellie teased, knowing full well that I believed in all that stuff.

"Don't mock. Everything happens for a reason, Ellie," I reminded her. "Synchronicities are everywhere."

"I'm not sure spirits have the ability to move objects," Spencer added.

"Why not? It's all energy. Just because our energy leaves our bodies when we pass, doesn't mean the energy stops moving."

"So you think that the energy of every living creature on this earth continues to move even once we're dead?" Spencer didn't look convinced.

"Well, not forever, no."

"How long, then?"

"A week, maybe two." I really had no idea of the answer or even if my theory had any science-based evidence, but I'd watched Tyler Henry, and I liked the idea that Emily could still be around. "Maybe we need a medium?" The thought brightened me, and I took the last few steps two at a time.

Glancing over my shoulder, I saw Spencer roll his eyes and smile at Ellie. They didn't believe. Which was fine, as everyone was entitled to their own beliefs. They just needed to be enlightened.

"I'm going to quickly drop my bag in my room," Ellie announced, her hand on the door.

"That's not your room," Spencer quipped.

"Huh?" Ellie looked at the small number printed on the door. "Darn it. Nancy's door looks exactly like mine. I'm going to leave a note in the suggestion box that they paint the doors different colors, so I can easily tell which one is which."

I grinned back at her as she moved to the correct door.

Reaching my room, I unlocked the door and dropped my bag on the bed as I raced to the desk, moving three notebooks that had been dropped on top of what I was looking for.

Carefully prying the screwed-up paper apart, I noted how it had dried overnight, and I was now worried I might rip it, but I managed to smooth it out without too much damage.

"I think there's more than one page there." Spencer took the paper from me and turned it over, peeling a second page from the back as Ellie entered the room.

"What do you think it's from?" she asked, rushing toward us.

"The writing's hard to read, but my guess is it's been torn from a notebook." Spencer pointed to the tiny holes down the left edge of the page. "Looks spiral bound to me."

"What are you thinking, Aubrey?" Ellie asked, flopping onto my bed.

"What if Willow was holding it when she fell?"

"Why would she be holding half a page?" Ellie asked.

I shrugged.

"Can we make out the writing?" Ellie sat wide-eyed as I compared it to the photo I had of Willow's handwriting.

It didn't match. So, this wasn't a note that Willow had written.

"Some words but nothing cohesive. The wet night air destroyed the integrity of it." Spencer sighed.

"That looks like it says something about flowers," I mused, pointing to some faded ink as I read over his shoulder. Would Chris have killed Willow over that?

"This note is nothing important." Spencer handed it to me and moved to sit in the chair beside the window.

"How do you know that?"

"No one would commit murder over flowers."

"Tell that to a wife who didn't get any on Valentine's Day," Ellie mused.

"Spencer, for a writer you have no imagination. How are your books so successful?" I asked.

"Because despite the fact I write fiction, I like it believable." Spencer shot a lopsided grin, his eyes gleaming with amusement.

I wanted to argue that my books were believable too, yet my imagination was very vivid but decided against it.

"I need to get this straight." Ellie propped a pillow behind her back and curled her legs up on the mattress. "We believe Willow was holding this paper as she was pushed to her death?"

I nodded. "Possibly."

"Do we believe it's a coincidence or is relevant to our case?"

I shrugged.

Spencer rolled his eyes. "Ellie, it's not *our* case. Nor do we know it came from Willow's room. It could have blown in from anywhere."

She dismissed him with a wave of her hand.

"Spence, this hotel is the only building in a five-mile radius," I added. "What are the chances of it blowing in from anywhere?"

He leaned forward, his arms on his knees. "Okay, I'll agree it is most likely from someone in this hotel. That doesn't mean it's relevant to Willow."

He had a valid point, yet something was nagging at my intuition.

"But it was found beneath her window," I stated. "What was it doing there?"

"A squirrel probably found it by the trash and used it to build a nest."

I squinted at the words on the paper as I considered his argument.

"Let's assume it's relevant, and she was holding it. What was in the notebook it came from?" Ellie asked.

"What do you write in your notebooks?" Spencer asked us, his gaze falling to the one poking out of my bag.

"Everything," I replied.

"Ah, that explains why you're single-handedly keeping the stationery industry afloat." He smiled.

"Well, what do you use yours for?"

"Novels. I have a new one for every book I plan. It's tabbed, and I keep track of characters, ideas, chapter outlines."

Ellie gasped. "What if someone was trying to steal one of Willow's ideas? She caught them with her notebook, struggled to stop them, and fell."

"Yes!" I yelled. "That's it."

"Only you've just said it's not Willow's handwriting, and it doesn't explain the marks on her neck," Spencer countered. "Or the fact that you overheard Naomi and Chris, and you think Chris killed her."

I nodded. "You're right. Maybe my judgment is clouded, and I'm ignoring the fact that anyone could have been in Willow's room at that time. Maybe she was sitting on the window ledge getting some fresh air, and the perp entered her room. They fought over something, and she fell."

"The perp?" The corner of Spencer's lip quivered.

"It's important to use the correct terminology," I reminded him.

"If you say so." His smile flashed, and I had to steady myself.

"I wish we could see the book the page came from." Ellie furiously typed notes into her phone. "We'd know for sure then."

"It's probably nothing," Spencer added.

"Possibly, but it would be good to cross it off the list, regardless."

"Okay," Spencer interrupted. "Let's assume you're right, Ellie. Tate would have found the book, for sure."

"He never mentioned it to me," I added.

"And he divulges all his suspect information to you now, does he?" Spencer's lip curled as he cracked his knuckles.

"Only one way to find out." Ellie beamed, clicking off her phone and dropping it into her pocket. "Let's go for a look in Willow's room."

Spencer leaned forward and rested his elbows on his knees. "You're not thinking of looking *now*, are you?"

"Sure. Why not?"

"Because it's the middle of the afternoon. People are everywhere. Anyone could see you."

"Then we look tonight," I suggested. "Ellie, you and I can do the searching, and Spencer, will you be our lookout? If you see or hear anyone heading toward Willow's room, you can text us, and we'll hide."

Spencer groaned, but he didn't say no.

* * *

Luckily, when I packed for the weekend, I'd thought to bring a boring black hoodie and jeans. True, I'd never imagined I would have been wearing them for my very first full-blown B&E, but it was good to know I was prepared for any occasion.

"Ready?" Ellie asked, standing in front of the mirror in my room and zipping up her hoodie that looked very similar to mine.

My muscles felt a bit twitchy, and I was perspiring more than normal, but I at least had the outfit right. "As I'll ever be."

"Can I just reiterate that I think this is a stupid idea?" Spencer stood with his hands on his hips, his eyebrows lowered as he stared down at us.

"You can, but it's not going to change anything." I flipped up my hood, covering my head. "I'm still going to search Willow's room."

"You'd look far less suspicious if you were dressed normally," he added, rolling his eyes.

"We'll blend into the darkness this way," Ellie added.

Spencer sighed, perching on the edge of my bed. "Alright, but I'd feel better if you let me search the room and you both do the lookout."

"That's a lovely offer, Spence, but this was my idea, so I should be the one doing it," I explained, ignoring the twists in my belly.

"Yeah, and I trust you a whole lot more on lookout than I do Aubrey," Ellie finished.

He lifted his hands to surrender. "All right, then be safe. I'll stay on the second floor and will message you if anyone looks like they're heading up. Keep your phone's flashlight on low, so it doesn't alert anyone outside that you could be snooping around in there."

I nodded, changing the setting as advised.

"Come on. Let's go." Ellie grabbed my arm before opening my door. Surreptitiously checking the hallway for anyone who might be lurking, she stepped onto the landing. I followed her closely, with Spencer right behind me. We quietly crept toward the stairs, the dim overhead bulb lighting our way. Spencer stopped, took a seat on a hard uncomfortable chair, and placed his book on the side table alongside the bronze statue of a headless man.

"Why are male statues so often naked?" I asked, assessing the anatomical correctness of it and thinking whoever the sculptor was had obviously been overcompensating for something.

Spencer glanced toward it but chose not to answer. Instead, he turned to Ellie and me and asked, "Are your phones on silent mode?"

I refocused, double-checked my phone, and nodded as Ellie took the first step leading up. It creaked under her weight, and I winced. She froze.

Thankfully, no one stepped out of their rooms to see what was going on, so we continued our ascent.

The light faded behind us as we reached the top floor, and as much as I wanted to flip the overhead light switch, I instead aimed my flashlight at the crime scene tape pinned across Willow's bedroom door.

"Ellie, should we be wearing gloves?"

"I hadn't thought of that. Do you think the police would have dusted for prints already?"

I shrugged and hurriedly messaged Spencer. His response was he thought we'd be fine but maybe keep our hands to ourselves as much as possible and definitely don't touch the window latch.

With the all clear, I took a deep calming breath and followed Ellie as she pushed the police tape aside and turned the handle. A shiver ran down my spine when the old door creaked open, the moonlight pouring in through the window and giving the room an eerie glow.

Stepping inside, I could honestly say I had never been in a turret before, but this one didn't disappoint. Five windows were dotted evenly amongst the whitewashed walls that circled around us. The pitch of the dark wood ceiling stopped at a point high above, and a metal chandelier hung from oppressive beams over the king-size bed.

As I swept my light around the room, I noted that Willow was particularly untidy. Or maybe the police had done that when they searched the room. Clothes were strewn across the bed, her suitcase left open on the stand near one of the windows. Shoes were left as if she'd just stepped out of them, and a pale pink Ted Baker longline peacoat was flung over the back of a velvet studded armchair. I recognized the coat immediately as I'd Google searched it the second I'd seen Willow enter the retreat wearing it. It was gorgeous, and I now stopped myself from rushing toward it and running my fingers over the soft cashmere.

"I can still smell Willow's perfume in here," Ellie commented quietly.

"That's because the bottle's broken." Shards of broken glass glittered in the moonlight, and the amber aroma of Coco

Mademoiselle tickled my senses. I moved my flashlight to illuminate my point.

"I wonder how that happened?"

"Maybe Willow was holding it when her attacker caught her off guard?" My mind flashed over possibilities. "Or maybe that was the thump I heard last night. You don't think her ghost will be hanging around, do you?"

"I don't believe in such things."

"I'll convert you. Don't you worry." I gripped the back of her hoodie for comfort.

"No way. If I believe, then they could quite possibly show up. So, I'm going for the non-believer attitude and explaining every strange sound with science. And besides, it's far more likely that someone came into this room last night and knocked it over. Now, why don't you start searching her wardrobe, and I'll look in the bathroom," Ellie suggested.

"Why would she have a notebook in the bathroom?"

"She might have been reading in the bath."

"True. But why don't you take the wardrobe, and I'll look in the bathroom?" I swung my light over the foreboding cupboard, and a chill danced down my spine. I suddenly liked Ellie's option better.

"Because it looks creepy, and I don't want to be anywhere near it. And as this was your idea then it's only fair that you're the one to search the scariest places."

Geez, I never could argue with her logic.

Reluctantly letting go of her, I took some security in the knowledge that, as my room was directly below, no one else should hear any of our footsteps. But better to be safe than sorry, so I tiptoed as quietly as I could.

Bypassing the unmade bed, I stopped in front of the heavy mahogany cupboard, gulping as it loomed dark and imposing. The scarred door was ajar, highlighting the blackness within. I shivered as the moonlight disappeared behind a cloud and threw the room into darkness. Clutching my phone as if my life depended on it, I bit my lip, rethinking my bright idea to search the room. I mean, the amount of clothing that was thrown around indicated Willow had never even used the wardrobe, so what was the point of checking?

"Hey, Ellie!" I dashed to the bathroom, my heart rate settling slightly as Ellie turned to stare at me.

"I think we should leave this to the police," I rushed. "I mean, it's really none of our business, is it? Let's leave it up to Tate to solve the mystery."

Ellie tilted her head as her breath rushed toward me. "Stop being a scaredy cat. Would your characters act this way? Or would they be brave and do the job they needed to do in order to save their friend?"

"There's one big difference between me and my characters," I reminded her. "It's fact versus fiction. If I write that my character gets attacked by a ghost, no one really gets hurt. But in reality, I can very much be haunted. And who's to say Willow's ghost won't attach itself to me, and then I carry it around for the rest of my life? Don't look at me like that." I flashed my light into Ellie's face. "I've seen it happen on Ghost Hunters."

"Aubrey, this was your idea!"

"Yes, but that was before I saw that wardrobe."

Ellie huffed. "Okay, but we've come too far to turn around and leave before we search the room. So, we'll stick together. Okay?"

I did feel better with Ellie alongside me, so I nodded my agreement.

"Great. Then let's go back into the bedroom and look in there," Ellie continued.

"Nothing in the bathroom?"

"No. Other than a few thousand dollars' worth of cosmetics that I can only dream of using."

Once in the bedroom, I followed Ellie as she hesitantly moved toward the wardrobe. I held my breath as one finger pulled the door open, and her flashlight scanned the interior.

"It's empty." She released a long breath.

Maybe Willow was as freaked out about it as we were.

Pointing her light toward the suitcase, Ellie said, "You look in there, and I'm going to go through Willow's satchel. I'm sure the police took her laptop, but maybe I can find something to access her files in the cloud."

"Jenna might know her username and password."

"Then when we're done here. I'll ask her," Ellie stated, her tone impatient.

Knowing when to shut up, I moved my attention to the suitcase, kneeling in front of it.

It didn't feel haunted, which settled the hair on the back of my neck. In fact, the suitcase was the opposite of scary. The champagne-colored leather trim complete with the Louis Vuitton logo was dreamy and in complete contrast to the black case I'd purchased from Walmart. Designer brands weren't exactly my thing—my wardrobe selection leaning more toward Target, but that was because my budget demanded it. Still, I could appreciate couture when I saw it.

I would have liked to admire it a little bit longer, but the moonlight snuck from behind the clouds and illuminated the room in an eerie glow. I shivered and hurriedly rifled through the clothing that remained in the case. Thankfully, someone before me had left it messed, so I didn't need to worry about being neat. I did, however, want to leave it the way I'd found it, and as I dropped a silk scarf onto the floor, I reached down to pick it up, forgetting about the broken perfume bottle. The sharp sting of glass cutting my hand caused a string of cursing.

"Aubrey! Keep it down," Ellie shushed. "We're not supposed to be here, remember?"

Wincing, I hurriedly sucked my finger, hoping to keep any of my blood from remaining at the crime scene.

"I cut myself," I whined as the perfume oozed into the wound, causing my eyes to tear up against the sting. "Geez Louise, it hurts!"

"Well, this might take your mind off it. I think I've found something hidden in a pocket under this satchel," Ellie muttered, gaining my full attention as she held up a notebook.

"How on earth did you find that?"

"I used to own a bag just like this one. It had the same secret pocket sewn into the bottom, making it look like part of the bag."

Ellie flipped a few pages, her phone light swaying across the handwriting.

"Is it the one we're looking for? What does it say?" I shoved my hand into the pocket of my jeans and moved to look over Ellie's shoulder.

"The handwriting is beautiful, but nothing like what's written on the ripped paper you found. Does it match the photo you took of Willow's handwriting?"

I hurriedly swiped at my phone and pulled up the photo in question. "Not really." I sighed. "Can you read any of the writing? In this light, I can barely make out a single word."

"It's very swirly. Aubrey! Hold the light still will you? It's hard enough to work this out without you swaying it around."

"Sorry. But the creaking and groaning coming from the ceiling is freaking me out. Can we take it and get out of here?" My eyes felt wide as I scanned the room for the bogeyman.

"We can't take it! It's not ours to take."

"Is it the only notebook that was in there?" I asked, a thrill of excitement buzzing in my belly.

"No. There're others, but this is the only one that was hidden. It could be the outline to a novel."

"Are there any torn pages?"

"I don't think so, but I can't tell in this light."

"So, we take them all to my room, read them thoroughly, and then return them once we've eliminated them from our investigation. It may not be what we're looking for, but we could still learn something. Ellie, I know what you're thinking, but I can't take photos of every page in an entire notebook."

"Fair point." She bit her lip, staring at the book in her hand. "We'll do what you suggested, read them thoroughly, and then forget any plots that Willow had planned," Ellie warned.

"Even though we believe that not to be her handwriting, what do you think I'll do with them? Take her *New York Times* best-selling ideas and write my next book based on them?" No matter how tempting that was, I had integrity.

"No." Ellie huffed out a breath, but I could see the indecision in her frown.

Giving her a moment, my gaze moved to the window and the car headlights that had pulled into the driveway.

"Kill your flashlight," I hissed, my fingers fumbling with my phone. "Someone just pulled in, and I don't want them to see we're in here."

Ellie hurriedly copied me, and seconds later, we were plunged into darkness as the moon had once again disappeared behind a cloud.

"Whose car was it?" Ellie asked, peering toward the window.

"No idea, but I really want to get out of here. It's making me beyond anxious." Adrenalin was causing my hand to shake and my feet to be restless.

"Yeah, okay. Come on." Fabric rustled in the darkness as Ellie tucked the books under her arm. I reached out to hold the back of her hoodie as we crossed the room. Ellie opened the door and stepped over the police tape, and light from the downstairs landing illuminated the staircase.

I had one leg either side of the police tape strung across the door as Spencer's voice boomed toward us.

"So, what brings you here at this time of the evening, Detective Tate?"

I felt Ellie stiffen as she stopped, and I almost fell into her.

"Something has come to my attention that I want to double-check at the crime scene. What about you? That looks like a very uncomfortable chair to sit and read in."

Spencer laughed, and Ellie grabbed my arm, pushing me backwards into the room.

"No," I whispered as loudly as I dared. "We can't. Tate'll be going in there." I'd already been stuck in a situation similar earlier and didn't want to repeat it.

"What other options do we have?" Hysteria laced her breath.

Beats me, but as the only hiding place in Willow's room was that scary wardrobe, I hurriedly scanned the small landing. My gaze stopped on the closet.

"There! It'll be safer than the bedroom." Pushing past Ellie, I grabbed the handle as Tate said his goodbyes to Spencer and prepared to wedge myself and Ellie in, when Tate's footsteps echoed toward us.

I grabbed Ellie's arm and flung the closet door open. Pushing her in ahead of me, I quickly followed, closing it as quietly as I could.

Ellie stumbled backwards trying to move a box aside so both of us could fit.

"Shush," I warned, my heart rate in the stroke zone.

"The space is too small," she hissed.

I pressed my body close to hers, when the groan of wood complaining about the stress gave way to Ellie squealing and grabbing my arm. A cold gush of stale air rushed toward us and Ellie's weight toppled, almost pulling me over.

Stumbling after her, my arms grazed the close walls before my bearings were momentarily lost in the pitch black. I grabbed for anything to balance as it felt like the back of the closet was giving way and we were left tumbling after it, into the abyss.

What the…?

CHAPTER SEVEN

───

Pain shot through my chest, my knees shook, and I wondered if I'd peed my pants. Ellie clutched me tightly, her breathing coming so hard and fast that I worried the detective may hear us.

"I think we're in a stairwell," she whispered.

Thankfully, my death grip on the wall saved us both from falling into the unknown. My hearing was on high alert as she held me tightly in her grasp. Tate was obviously ascending the stairs as the sound of randomly creaking planks broke through the pounding of my blood pressure in my ears, and I prayed the sound had covered any noises we had made.

Fighting the urge to put my flashlight on, I waited for any indication he'd gone into Willow's room, whereby we could safely find a way out of our predicament.

It didn't take long before the click of a switch was followed by a blast of light from under the door, and I felt as much as heard Tate walk into the room.

I released the breath I was holding and found my flashlight. Blinking against the glare, Ellie and I stared around us, taking in the steep winding staircase below. Looking back toward the closet, it looked eerie with the back panel acting as a secret doorway. Well, that explained a lot.

"What the heck?" Ellie whispered, her eyes wide, her mouth gaping open.

"Well that wasn't on the blueprints I saw in the library." My breath was shallow as a surge of adrenalin tingled through my body. My hand clutched Ellie's arm as if my life depended on it, and thoughts of the detective finding us were long forgotten. "I guess we've solved how people were escaping without us seeing them. Where do you think it leads?"

Ellie shrugged. "Let's follow it."

"Seriously?"

"I dropped the notebooks." She pointed downwards, indicating their descent. "So, we kinda got to."

Not relishing the thought, I considered our options. "I guess it's better than waiting for Tate to find us. But I'm hiding behind you."

Silently as possible, I closed the back panel of the closet, hoping that if Tate did decide to look in there, he would only see what we'd previously believed it to be and not a secret passageway.

Willing the old spiral treads to cooperate in our escape, I followed Ellie in our descent, only stopping as she collected the notebooks.

The air was stale and cold, cobwebs dangled precariously above us, and the scent of musty stone walls clogged my sinuses as we navigated the tight space heading down. We stopped when we saw a door on our left.

"Wait!" I hissed as Ellie went to open it. My panicked breathing was loud in my ears. "Maybe we should keep going? We don't know what's on the other side."

"Who cares as long as it's not Tate?"

"True, but what if Nancy's out there nosing around? How do we explain this?"

My light cast Ellie's shadow against the door as she placed her ear to it. Nodding, she smiled tightly and then slowly turned the handle. My heart pounded as she checked her surroundings before stepping through the door.

"Ellie?" Spencer's voice was high, his surprise evident. "What the heck?"

Right behind her, I blinked in the bright light from the second-floor landing and stared into Spencer's pale face, my blood pressure instantly dropping into safer territory.

"How did you get there?" he gasped, rushing toward us, his hands pulling at his hair.

I didn't really know how to answer that, instead spinning to close the door behind us, noting the door to the stairs was completely concealed in the oak paneled wall.

Huh. I never would have guessed that was there.

Ellie's face was flushed as she brought Spencer up to speed, but before we could retreat to our rooms, Tate descended the stairs, catching us probably looking as guilty as sin.

"Aubrey." He was dressed in the same jeans and T-shirt that he'd been wearing that morning, only he'd changed his jacket. This one was tight across his biceps and skimmed his hips, highlighting his narrow waist. His eyes looked tired, but his smile was large and genuine.

"Hello, Detective," I trilled, doing my very best to look innocent. "Fancy meeting you here," I giggled, gaining myself a frown from both Ellie and Spencer. "I thought you'd be home in bed at this time of night."

Tate looked at his watch. "It's six-thirty."

Was it? Geez, it felt like midnight.

Ellie quickly recovered. "What are you doing here at this time of the *evening*?"

"I'm following up on a lead. Looking for some evidence." He held a notebook—the floral cover an exact match of the one we'd "borrowed." His eyes flicked toward the books under Ellie's arm, and the well-trodden *V* between his brows deepened.

Ellie audibly gulped and shuffled her feet, adjusting her stance.

"Where have you ladies been?" he asked, his sharp gray eyes scanning us before flicking to the wall panel we'd exited from.

"Ummm…" I blinked rapidly. Thinking fast on my feet wasn't a skill I possessed.

"We were having a plot meeting," Ellie lied.

Tate's eyebrow raised as his hand brushed my arm, dislodging some dust I'd collected from the narrow staircase. "Where exactly were you doing that?"

"The ahhhh… dining room." Ellie straightened her shoulders and fluttered her eyelashes.

"Huh. It seems the onsite manager needs to speak to housekeeping." Tate's fingers gently brushed my temple as he lifted a stray cobweb from my hair, and I shivered against his touch.

"That book looks very similar to the ones Willow used." He lifted the book in his spare hand for effect.

"Yes, well, they're standard Walmart stock. Always good value for money," Ellie explained, the tips of her ears reddening.

Tate nodded, yet his hand slipped down to mine, lifting it between his fingers. My cut skin tingled, and I jumped.

"You know what's strange?" he asked, his eyes locking on to mine. My heart rate kicked up a notch, and I almost hyperventilated.

"No," I squeaked.

"There were fresh drops of blood in Willow's room that weren't there this morning. And if I'm not mistaken..." He leaned in close and inhaled deeply. "You smell like Coco Mademoiselle."

"Yes, well, it's ummm... one of my favorites." Oh God. Breathe, Aubrey. Breathe. "Willow must have worn the same perfume that I do."

"How do you know I was going to say Willow wore that perfume?" He didn't miss a thing, did he?

"I, ummm... I surmised. From, you know, what you were inferring." I was having a few issues with my thought process, and Tate's suspicious stare wasn't helping matters.

"Detective," Spencer spoke up for the first time, his jaw tight. "If there's nothing we can help you with, would you excuse us? We have work to do."

Tate's gaze skimmed our group before he nodded. "Of course. You're welcome to go. Only I'd like to get Aubrey's cut seen to."

I reluctantly pulled my hand away from his. "It's nothing. Really. I just cut it on... ummm." Darn it. What did I cut it on?

"It's a paper cut," Ellie lied. I thought she was very convincing, yet Tate didn't look satisfied.

"Who knew paper could be so aggressive?" He chuckled low and sensual, and my ovaries nearly exploded.

"Oh, hahaha."

From the glare Ellie threw my way, I figured I sounded like an idiot. Spencer grunted and rolled his eyes. I hurriedly shut up.

Ellie cleared her throat. "You go and get your cut seen to, Aubrey, and we'll chat about plots when you're finished." Wordless conversation crossed the space between us, and I understood exactly what she meant. I only hoped they didn't uncover any juicy gossip without me.

* * *

"Really, you shouldn't have worried. Ouch!" I snatched my hand from Tate's grasp and gasped against the sting of antiseptic. I sat heavily on the nearby kitchen chair and winced.

"Sorry. I didn't mean to hurt you." His eyes softened as he took my fingers in his and gently wrapped a band-aid around my wound.

Tate had easily found the first-aid box under the kitchen sink and had taken it upon himself to dress my cut. I'd tried my best—okay, maybe not my *best*, but I had definitely tried—to stop him. Only as a homicide detective, he'd been very determined to patch me up, and how could I argue with a man like that?

And as his musky scent filled my senses, and the still evening air caused goosebumps to dance over my exposed skin, I'd pretty much lost all my ability to speak, so it was just easier to let him take care of me.

To be honest, it was very nice having a strong man take care of me for a moment, no matter how small my wound was. Sure, I was all into female empowerment and how women could look after themselves, but every now and then, it felt wonderful to be taken care of. For a moment, to have someone put you above everything else going on in their lives, filled me with warmth. True that heat shouldn't be traveling quite as far south as it was, but that was a side effect I was willing to endure.

Tate wrapped the Band-Aid into place and squeezed gently. "That's a serious paper cut you have. Maybe I should find the perpetrator and arrest him for grievous bodily harm." The corner of his lips twitched.

"Yes, well, I'll think twice before turning the page next time."

Coolness swept in as he dropped my hand and threw the rubbish in a nearby trash can.

"Every job comes with its dangers, Aubrey."

"Admittedly, the biggest danger being an author has posed to date is the damage it's done to my backside."

Tate's gaze flicked to my derriere, and heat flushed my cheeks. Oh geez. Why did I have to mention that? I mean, I could have said anything! Like, the cramp I got in my fingers as they flew across the keyboard.

Just as I thought my face would combust and set fire to the kitchen, his phone rang, the loud ringtone causing me to jump. He glanced at the screen, and his shoulders sank.

"Will you excuse me while I take this call, please?" Tate didn't wait for my response, instead standing and moving a few feet away. "Hi, Denise. Uh-huh... great."

My ears pricked up at the mention of the coroner's name. Thankfully, I had good hearing, and I covered my eavesdropping with a sudden intense interest in the gauze he'd used to clean my wound. I was sure I looked convincing.

"Can you give me the quick run-down?" Tate continued, his voice hushed. "Uh-huh.... yep... okay, so how many months pregnant was she?" He paused. "Four months. And the cause of death was cervical fracture compromising the neurological supply to the respiratory organs. The broken neck is consistent with the fall from the third-floor window?" He waited a beat before nodding. "Okay, well thanks for getting that processed so quickly. Yep, you too... goodnight."

Tate closed his eyes and pinched the bridge of his nose as the stark overhead lights highlighted dark rings under his eyes. His exhale was long and controlled.

"Sorry, I couldn't help but overhear..." I gulped as he lifted his chin, and his gaze connected with mine. Vulnerability flashed for a moment before he blinked, and his professional demeanor once again masked his true feelings.

"Willow was pregnant?" I pushed.

He stared at me for a moment before nodding.

"Do you know who the father was?" I asked.

From his slow breath and pensive expression, I got the idea he was having an internal debate about whether to share with me.

After a moment, he released a sigh and said, "I'm going with Jonathan Berkley, as he was her partner. Unless you know something I don't." A mischievous glint sparkled in his eyes.

"Why would I know something like that?" A delicious low hum vibrated in my belly as Tate crossed the room and sat on the chair alongside me, his knees stopping inches from mine. He sure took up a lot of air space.

"You seem like a very resourceful woman." His gaze was filled with warmth. "Ever thought of being a detective?"

"I'm not brave enough to be a detective."

"You're nosy enough." His grin belied his teasing.

"I'm going to pretend I didn't hear that." I huffed indignantly, yet the tingles that danced down my spine almost took my breath away.

His laugh was short and full of humor. "Seriously, you knew Willow better than I did. You know the people who surrounded her. You hear the gossip."

"You overestimate me."

"I don't think so." His smile grew. "So come on. Do you agree with me that the baby's father was likely Berkley?"

I bit my lip, considering telling him what I knew. "The evidence would suggest that, but I'm not so sure as I saw him in an interview for men's health, and he said he never wanted kids." I shrugged. "I guess it could have been an accident."

"Or not."

I raised an eyebrow questioningly.

"Some women have their ways to get what they want," Tate challenged.

My gasp defended all the honest women in the world.

Tate lifted his hands in surrender. "Hey, I come across a lot of not so nice people. I've known a lot of women who have used a pregnancy to get control over someone."

"That's terrible."

"Yeah, it really is. But women manipulating men with their sexuality has been going on for millennia."

"Men do it too."

Tate's shoulders dropped. "I know. And it's wrong. All of it. But that doesn't stop it from happening."

I sat and considered his following silence, wondering if it was personal experience or just from the job. However, as much as I wanted the answer, I never asked the question.

"If the baby was Jonathan Berkley's, and he didn't want it, could that give him motive to kill Willow?" I asked instead.

"Pushing someone out of a window is a very drastic way of eliminating an unwanted child. If the killer knew about the pregnancy, then they could be looking at two counts of murder."

That definitely put a new spin on things. "He's here, you know. Berkley. He's been here the entire time, hiding out from everyone. He easily could have been in Willow's room waiting for her to return."

"Have you seen him?"

"No, he's very elusive. Makes him very suspicious if you ask me."

"But it doesn't make him guilty of murder."

"An explanation wouldn't go astray though, right?"

"If you see him, please do not approach him and pepper him with questions. Let me do my job."

My hand flew to my chest. "What are you insinuating?"

"That you're interfering in my investigation."

"I would never!"

Tate held my stare, and my heart missed a thousand beats.

"So, tell me, Aubrey. The truth. You cut your hand in Willow's room tonight, didn't you?"

I did a very good impression of a goldfish, my mouth opening and closing repeatedly on a loop.

"The only part I can't figure out is how you escaped without me catching you."

Choosing not to respond, I pulled my gaze away, knowing if he looked into my soul long enough, I would cave and tell him everything. Which could get me into a lot of trouble.

"Don't worry." He grinned. "I'm not going to arrest you for entering a crime scene. I've done my homework on you, and I gather—no matter what I tell you to do—you'll do what you want anyway."

"Why did you investigate me?"

"You were friends with my number one suspect. You found the body. I needed to know you weren't covering anything up for her."

My shoulders sank along with my heart. But then, he did say he wasn't going to arrest me.

"What did you learn about me?" I mean, how deep did a homicide detective dig?

Heat burned my ears as Tate leaned backwards, his gaze intent before his eyes turned sad.

I gulped, wishing I could retract my question.

"You found out about Emily?" My voice dropped to a whisper.

Tate nodded. "Yeah. The accident came up. I'm sorry, Aubrey. Losing someone that close is hard."

"You know from personal experience?"

"Only interviewing families. It's not a part of the job I enjoy."

"Which part do you enjoy?"

"The bit where I can look the victims' loved ones in the eye and tell them we've made an arrest."

"Yeah, I guess that makes up for the crappy part." I wanted to move the conversation in a new direction. Because I'd learned I was just as uncomfortable talking about Emily as everyone else seemed to be. "Did you learn anything good about me?"

Tate grinned, and the previous awkwardness instantly dissolved.

"You're hard working, and when you get your teeth into something, you're like a dog with a bone." He leaned forward into my air space, the color of his eyes deepening as his smile disappeared. "But Aubrey, Willow's case isn't fiction. There's a real killer among us. Believe me when I say I don't want to be investigating your murder too."

I gulped. When he put it like that.

"So if I'd learned anything useful I could share this information and not be punished?" Even though a night in his handcuffs did seem appealing.

"Your secrets are safe with me."

I took a moment to think this through, wondering if I should tell him about the hidden stairs.

"All I know for sure is what I've already told you." I leaned back and bit my lip, jumbled thoughts fighting for first place. "Even though… I think Chris is a very good candidate for the murderer. He had the means. Pushing someone out a window is pretty easy. He had the opportunity as I saw him on the front stairs when I was exiting the building right before finding her body, but I'm unsure if that gave him enough time to commit murder and then casually walk away."

"Maybe, but what was his motive?"

I shrugged. "Willow was letting him read her manuscripts, and it was very secretive, but that could have been because she didn't trust many not to steal it. Naomi knows he did something to Willow, only I don't know what and whether it's even related. I also overheard a conversation between Willow and Levi where she told him to leave because she had a restraining order. Only he didn't look homicidal. He looked sad that they were no longer together. Plus, he was crying when we spoke to him later that night in the dining room. He looked devastated, not like a killer. Ricky was here wanting to speak to Willow, but he left once Jenna escorted him from the property. Oh! Apparently, Willow was going to fire Naomi once the weekend was over. And Naomi was in the kitchen right after I heard someone in Willow's room last night. Naomi said she was on the phone to her mom, but whose mom wants to hear gossip at one in the morning?"

Tate sat back against the chair, his eyes wide.

"Not mine, that's for sure," I continued, seemingly unable to stop.

"Wait!" Tate held up a hand. "Someone was in Willow's room?"

"Uh-huh. I heard them, but when I got to the bottom of the stairs to see who it was, no one appeared. I now think they knew about the secret passage. Only who would know about that? Chris maybe? He is the manager here after all and would know the secrets the building held." It seemed I had diarrhea of the mouth.

"Secret passage?"

I stopped as heat flushed my face. I'd said way more than I had intended. "You're very good at your job," I mumbled, dropping my gaze to my hands.

"Aubrey."

"Yes?"

"Aubrey, look at me."

"I don't want to."

"You're not in trouble. I just want to know everything that's been going on. Please."

I reluctantly lifted my eyes to meet his, expecting to see annoyance brimming in their smoky gray depths. Instead, I found them soft and anchored on mine.

"There's… there's a secret set of stairs that lead down from the turret," I mumbled.

"And you know this, how?"

"I found them."

His eyebrows got lost around his hairline.

I took a deep breath and decided I needed to tell him everything. By the time I'd finished, he was sitting back with his arms crossed over his chest, looking very much like a homicide detective.

"Where exactly are these stairs?" he asked, his waning patience visible in the firm line of his lips.

"Maybe it would be easier to show you."

Tate pushed back his chair and stood, indicating I should lead the way. Passing the dining room, I gazed in to see Ellie and Spencer deep in conversation, their heads low over the notebook. I guess I hadn't told Tate everything after all.

The air was still and quiet as we made our way up to the second-floor landing, only stopping outside the door to Berkley's room.

"If he's innocent, why do you think he's hiding out?" I asked, coming to an abrupt halt. Tate nearly walked into the back of me.

"I don't know he is hiding out. But if he is, believe me, I will find him."

I gulped, not denying a single syllable.

Continuing on in silence, I led the way up to the turret. The small landing felt so much smaller with Tate alongside me. His body heat radiated across the space. Ignoring my racing pulse, I pulled open the closet door and flipped the light switch on.

Musty air gushed out toward us, a slight breeze propelling it forward. Stray cobwebs clung to the single bulb hanging from the overhead cord, illuminating the dust particles dangling like tendrils in front of me. I shivered.

Tate looked over my shoulder, deep lines appearing on his brow.

"It's a broom closet."

"That's what we thought. But look." Pushing the back panel, the secret entrance opened, and Tate looked suitably impressed.

"Lead the way." He tapped at the screen of his phone, and the flashlight illuminated the path ahead. I copied him.

He stayed close behind me as I made my descent, noting my heart rate was a lot lower this time. As his breath tickled my neck, I realized it wasn't actually all that much.

Reaching the doorway that led to the second-floor landing, I paused. "This is where we exited."

"Right before I saw you?"

"Uh-huh."

"Okay. Then let's keep going. See where it leads."

"Sure. But can I follow you?" It had been one thing leading the way when I knew where I was going, but venturing into the unknown was a whole different matter.

"Really? You made it this far the first time without being scared."

"Oh, I was scared. But it was a fear of you putting me in handcuffs that propelled me forward. That dark stairwell could be home to ghosts for all I know."

"Do you want to get out here? I'll come and find you once I'm done."

His body had pushed up against mine, his heat filling me with comfort and safety. I took a moment to think things through.

"Do you have a gun?" I asked, turning my own flashlight toward him as I scanned his body for a weapon.

"Yes." He tapped his jacket. "But it won't protect you from the bogeyman if that's what you're wondering."

"The bogeyman? Oh geez. Why did you have to put that thought in my mind?"

His chuckle was low in his throat. "Seriously, Aubrey. Hop out here. I'll find you when I'm done."

"No. It's okay. I'm brave." Nosy was a better description. I really did want to know where this staircase led.

"If you say so."

Choosing to ignore his implied meaning, I continued on. My hand trailed against the stone walls as the stairs wound downwards, tight, and narrow, the air musty and stale. The narrow wooden treads strained beneath my feet, and I slipped against the tight turn. My backside hit the tread, and I squealed as I slid, only stopping as I slammed into a wood panel that gave way as my weight hit it. Tumbling out, I landed flat on my back, slightly winded.

Urgh! Maybe it was time to reassess my life choices.

CHAPTER EIGHT

Tate's strong hand cradled my face, his searching look rapidly scanning my body. "Aubrey, are you hurt?"

I mentally checked myself for injuries, touched by his genuine concern.

"Only my pride," I mumbled as he sat back on his haunches and grinned. Accepting Tate's outstretched hand, I allowed him to pull me to my feet, taking in my surroundings. I saw Ellie and Spencer hurry across the dining room toward me.

"What are you doing?" Spencer asked, his gaze making me very conscious of the fact that my hoodie had ridden up and I was showing more midriff than I was comfortable with.

Pulling my clothing back into place, I noted Tate was now assessing the old staircase.

"The detective and I were checking out where that led." I pointed toward the wall panel that had hidden the stairs.

Ellie's eyes moved from side to side rapidly, and I could see her thought process written in the deep *V* between her brows.

"I told him everything," I confessed, wiping dust from my jeans.

What? she mouthed, her eyes wide.

"He interrogated me. What was I to do? I could hardly lie to a police officer!"

Spencer rubbed the back of his neck, tension evident in his shoulders as he shifted his weight from one foot to the other.

"So, you told him that we were in Willow's room?" Ellie whispered.

"Uh-huh."

"And that we took the notebooks?"

"Well, not that bit."

Tate's ears visibly twitched. "Notebooks? So those books I saw you with were from her room?"

Ellie's face flushed, her features frozen.

"Aubrey, what else have you not told me?" Tate's tone was sharp.

"Nothing," I confessed. "And before you accuse me of withholding information, I was going to tell you about them. I just hadn't got to that part yet."

His eyes narrowed as they pinned me to the spot.

"Looks like we've reached that part now," mumbled Spencer.

"Start talking," Tate demanded.

"Can I sit down first? I think I've bruised my coccyx."

Compassion momentarily pushed his cop face aside before he dashed across the room and held a chair out for me. I wanted to believe he was doing it to help me, but I kind of felt it was more about speeding up our conversation.

My steps were slow as I hobbled toward him, noting Spencer's rigid movements as blood drained from Ellie's face with every step.

Wincing, I sat on the chair and took a slow breath. "How would I know if I'd broken something?" I stalled.

"I have my first aid certificate." Spencer's brow lowered as his gaze flicked to my butt. He briefly hesitated before saying, "I can take a look at it for you."

Now there was an offer I probably shouldn't refuse.

Tate's jaw ground as he glared at Spencer. "Do you need me to call a paramedic?" he asked me.

"No, thank you! I'm sure it's fine." As much as the fantasy of all these men looking at my derriere seemed appealing, the reality was much more embarrassing.

"Great. Now what is this about the notebooks you took from my crime scene?" Tate asked.

"We didn't take them! We just 'borrowed' them." I used air quotes to emphasize my point.

Tate took a long, controlled breath. "And what do they contain?"

"They're outlines for novels." Ellie squirmed uncomfortably.

"Then why are they important enough for you to 'borrow' them?" Tate copied my air quotes.

"Because we were hoping one of them would belong to the ripped page," I finished.

Tate's eyebrows almost hit his hairline.

I released a long deep breath before fully explaining why we were in Willow's room. By the time I'd finished, Tate's face was red, and he was taking his own deep breaths.

"So," he said, his voice tight, "did the page belong to the notebooks you found?"

I looked to Ellie and Spencer for confirmation.

"We don't think so," Ellie explained. "None of them seem to have any damage at all."

"You need to give it all to me and let the police do the work from now on."

"I'll grab them for you." Spencer's shoulders were tense and his step purposeful as he strode toward the dining table.

Ellie pulled her phone from her jacket pocket and opened her notes. As she furiously tapped at the screen, a thought hit me.

"Oh, Ellie. Did you know that Willow was pregnant?" I whispered.

Tate seemed to have supersonic hearing as he looked at me and groaned. "Seriously, Aubrey? That was confidential information."

Heat flushed my face. "Sorry, but Ellie and Spencer have been helping me investigate. Ellie has all the notes typed up and is keeping track of our suspects."

Tate pinched the bridge of his nose. Releasing a long breath, he pulled out a chair alongside me and sat down heavily. "I seriously think you'd better tell me everything. And I mean everything!"

Geez, he sure looked irritated.

"Well… I have told you everything."

"Really? This *investigation* is news to me."

"Investigation may be the wrong word," Ellie interjected. "We've been keeping a list of ideas."

"Then lay your ideas on me." His hand slapped the table, and I gulped.

Ellie sat at the table opposite and grimaced before reading her notes. Most of which I had already told Tate about.

"So do we think that Berkley was the baby daddy?" Ellie asked once Tate was caught up.

Spencer moved back toward us and handed the notebooks to Tate, who immediately started to look through them.

"Or maybe it was Levi," Ellie continued. "He was the jilted lover. Maybe Willow wouldn't let him be a part of the child's life. It could have been the real reason he was with her just before she died."

"His love seemed genuine," I mused.

Tate shifted, and a folded piece of paper slid from the back of a notebook and onto the floor at his feet. "What's this?" he asked.

I leaned forward to retrieve it for him when he did the same. The loud *thunk* as our skulls collided reverberated in my ears.

"Owww," I cried.

"Oh, geez. Sorry, Aubrey," Tate replied.

Ellie giggled.

Spencer scoffed.

"Are you okay?" Tate asked me as I rubbed the spot on my head that throbbed.

"Yep. But you sure have a hard head."

"You're not the first person to tell me that." Tate grinned, and I figured his bump didn't hurt as much as mine. He then bent forward and retrieved the paper, his long fingers effortlessly unfolding it. I watched as his smoky gray eyes scanned the handwriting before stopping on the last words.

"What is it?" I leaned in close, and his heat reached across the space between us.

Checking the page he held open, I noticed the flowery script written in the margin. "That's the same handwriting that's on the torn page I have! The rest of it's different though."

"Are you sure?" Tate's eyes looked into mine, and the simmering annoyance they'd previously held disappeared.

"About ninety-eight-point five percent." I nodded. "The page I have is quite damaged, but those *P*'s are very distinctive. What do you think this is?"

"Without further investigation, I have no idea."

"It looks like a chapter from a book. And the editor has some thoughts about it." Ellie pointed to the margin notes. "Can you check paper for fingerprints to see who it belongs to?"

"Yes," I cut in.

Spencer huffed out a breath. For some reason, I seemed to be irritating him.

Ignoring him, I pushed on. "Silver nitrate reacts with sodium chloride, aka salt, that's in your fingerprints. It forms a deposit of silver chloride which changes to dark brown or black under UV light."

Tate grinned. "Very good, Aubrey."

I shrugged, secretly pleased. "I researched it for a story. It's how they found the killer."

"I'll talk to the lab and see what they can do," Tate explained, folding the letter back up and placing it where it came from. "But I'll start with getting some handwriting samples. Would you mind going first Spencer?"

He stiffened. "You think I wrote it?"

"I need to eliminate everyone from the investigation. Someone has to go first. Write the words 'I love you.'" He pinned Spencer with a stare.

Spencer returned the look.

"So that I can compare the two samples—word for word," Tate finished, a mischievous twinkle in his eye. It appeared there wasn't a lot of love lost between these two men.

Spencer ground his teeth but snatched the pen Tate offered him before scribbling in the detective's notepad. Once he was finished, he almost threw it all on the table.

"If that's all," he growled, "I think it's time we wrap tonight up. Detective, we'll leave the investigation to you from now on. You seem to have everything under control."

"That's a very good idea," Tate responded, suppressing a grin. "But I'll need that torn page."

"It's in my room," I said.

"Don't worry, Aubrey," Spencer cut in. "I'll get it for you. You look like you're in a bit of pain after that fall. Do you have your room key?"

Ignoring the tension building between the men, I wrote *I love you* before passing the notebook to Ellie.

"It's not locked," I said to Spencer as Tate scowled in my direction. "I wanted to make sure we could duck back into my room in a hurry. You know, on the off chance we needed a fast get away. The evening didn't exactly go as planned."

"That's why you should leave the detective work to the detective," Tate growled. "But don't worry about the page tonight. I'll pick it up in the morning."

"Will you keep us updated?" I was ever hopeful.

"I can't make any promises. I will share what I can. But"—Tate narrowed his eyes and glanced at the three of us in turn—"you have to stay out of it now. I appreciate what you've told me, and I will repeat what I said earlier. There's a real murderer here. One that has already killed once, and from my past experience, I doubt they'd think twice before killing again if they believe they're being threatened. Which means that as long as you keep out of it, you'll be safe. I don't want the body count to increase. Okay?"

We all nodded solemnly as footsteps sounded on the boards in the hall. I looked over my shoulder to see Nancy staring at us, her brown eyes wide.

"Oh, hello. Am I interrupting anything?"

"No. Nothing important," Tate replied, standing.

Nancy smiled as Tate tucked the letter back into the notebook and placed it all under his arm.

"Now if you'll excuse me, I'll say goodnight." With one final tiny smile in my direction, he made his way from the room.

It was the sway of his hips and the sight of his jeans hugging his backside that would get me through the night.

As Nancy's gaze followed him, I figured she'd be having the same dreams as I would be.

* * *

I said goodnight to both Ellie and Spencer and headed to bed. My body felt stiff and sore, and I needed a hot shower.

As I was making my way along the hallway toward my room, Chris's hushed voice caught my attention from behind his half-closed office door.

"What do you mean you're going to tell Isla?" His voice was hard, his tone filled with venom.

I gasped and pushed myself close to the wall, eavesdropping at its best.

"If you whisper even a word of that to her... what? You'll do what, exactly? ... I'm not paying you anything until I know I can trust you... uh-huh... fine. Meet me in the old stable. See you in five." His sigh was loud and angry as he stomped across the room.

Who was going to tell Isla what? What were they going to do? And what exactly would Chris do to stop them?

As his footsteps neared, I made the hasty decision to hide in the nearest closet then follow him into the night.

CHAPTER NINE

I didn't have time to grab a jacket before I slid outside to follow Chris, and it wasn't long before the cold frosty air bit into my hoodie. My breath rose in thin silvery wisps as the wind blew up from the lake, and I rubbed my arms, wishing I'd had time to do things differently.

Chris strode ahead of me, his steps filled with purpose as he crossed the sprawling lawn. I watched from behind the boxwood hedge, only following him once he'd disappeared behind the fully grown western red cedar.

Glancing behind me, I ran across the frost hardened grass, my path illuminated by the occasional flicker of moonlight breaking through the clouds. As I reached the tree, I hugged the shadows and peered around the trunk just as Chris opened the arched door of the once grand stable. Now, the sturdy structure showed signs of age with vegetation encroaching on the walls and ivy winding its way through the broken windows.

Once Chris moved inside, I dashed across the gravel path, hoping he didn't hear me, and clung to the stone wall, daring to peer in through the dusty window.

It didn't take long to spot him standing on the dirt flooring, Ricky's large smile beaming back at him.

As my blood pounded loudly in my ears, making it difficult to hear anything, I decided to switch my phone to record and pushed the end through a broken pane of glass, hoping it would catch anything that I missed.

"Listen, I've had enough of all of this," Chris spat, causing me to jump. "First Naomi and now you! What do you want from me?"

"I know what you did to Willow. And I want money to keep quiet about it."

Chris scoffed. "You're an idiot."

"Call me any names you like, but unless you pay me what I want, then I tell Isla."

"What exactly do you think I did to Willow?"

Ricky crossed his arms, his gaze locked onto Chris. "You were having an affair with her. Don't deny it."

I smothered a gasp. Geez Louise, how did Willow have time for all these men and still write best-selling novels?

After a beat, Chris responded, "You don't know what you're talking about."

"Oh, but I do. Willow purchasing this property and making you the manager was all your idea. It gave you both so many opportunities to be alone without Isla listening in."

Chris scoffed. "Willow lived in California. She could hardly pop in when she felt like it."

"No, but from what I've heard, she sure loved a weekend getaway."

Chris crossed his arms and stared at Ricky. "Willow bought the place to escape the hustle and bustle. She loved coming here and enjoying the quiet life."

"The quiet life?" Ricky laughed. "I'm not sure that's what she was enjoying."

I slowly straightened my back and put my hand to the glass, willing my hearing to pick up on every sound. The secret life of Willow was enthralling.

"I don't know where you got your information from, but you're wrong," Chris finished.

"I'm not divulging my source, but I can tell you that it's someone close to Willow. Someone who knew everything she did. It's credible."

My mind jumped to Naomi. After all, a PA should know your schedule better than you do. But why would she tell Ricky?

"You've got nothing more than rumors," Chris spat.

"If that's true, then why did you run here to meet me so quickly?" Ricky's smile was slow and deliberate.

Chris faltered.

"What would happen if Isla learned the truth about you and Willow?" Ricky rocked back on his heels. A smug smile played on his lips, only his body tensed as if he was ready to defend himself. "Can't imagine she'd be happy about it."

Chris's chest rose and fell at a rapid rate. "Isla won't believe you."

"Oh, you're so wrong. She already knows Willow was pregnant. If I tell her about the affair, she may just come to conclusions on her own. Wouldn't look great for you, would it?"

"What? Willow was pregnant?" Chris shook his head.

"That's what I heard. Now Chris, are you the baby's daddy?"

Chris flinched as if he'd been slapped then stumbled backwards. His legs bumped an upturned barrel, and he sat down hard onto it. "I…no. There's no way that I'm the father. It's not possible." He stooped forward, his leg jiggling as he rubbed his brow.

"Anything's possible," Ricky pushed, either unaware of the distress Chris was feeling, or he didn't care.

"No… no! It's not. It's not. I'll never be a father. The doctors told me that."

"Maybe they were wrong. Either way, Isla's not going to be happy with you."

Chris hurriedly stood. "You can't tell her. Please. It'll destroy her. I've already killed her chances at being a mother. Don't do that to her."

"Shame you didn't think of that when you were doing the dirty with her sister," Ricky sneered. "What I don't understand is, if Isla's such a great woman, why would you risk your marriage in the first place?"

"Because I loved Willow."

"Then why didn't you do the right thing and leave Isla to be with her?"

"I wanted to, but Willow wouldn't let me! She didn't want me the same way I wanted her. In the beginning I loved Isla too, but do you know what years of IVF and trying for a baby does to a marriage? It destroys it." His voice cracked slightly on the last word, but there was something off about the way he said it—more frustration than grief. "I'm sorry for what I did, but please, Isla's hurting enough. I can't hurt her anymore."

"Convenient, though, isn't it?" Ricky's voice was low and cutting. "Willow dying the way she did. If I hadn't figured it out, your secret could very well have died with her."

Chris's words were like razors as he stood to face Ricky. "What exactly are you accusing me of?"

"I'm not accusing you of anything." Ricky held his hands up in surrender. "I'm just saying it looks bad. Willow winds up dead, and all your problems conveniently disappear."

"That's enough," Chris hissed. "You have no idea what you're talking about. But if you keep throwing around accusations like that, you're going to regret it."

He then pivoted on his heel and left Ricky staring after him. As he passed me on the way out the door, I held my breath and slunk back into the shadows, praying the moon didn't choose that moment to make an appearance.

* * *

Once I was safely in my room, I tried to settle for the night. Only there was no way I could slow my mind.

Was Chris's affair with Willow the reason she shared her manuscript with him? Was he the father of her child? Or was he telling the truth and was the reason for the IVF?

I texted both Ellie and Spencer, and then I made a few notes while I waited for them to come to my room.

A few minutes later, Ellie was propped on my bed, and Spencer was sitting on the chair in the corner of the room.

"Okay, spill," said Ellie, her eyes wide. "Your message sounded intense."

I took a deep breath, trying to organize my thoughts. "I followed Chris to the stable tonight. He was meeting Ricky."

Ellie leaned forward, her expression serious. "And?"

I hurriedly replayed my evening escapades for them. When I'd finished my story about Chris, Spencer was frowning, staring at his hands, and Ellie was biting her lip.

"Do you think Chris knew you were there?" Spencer asked, a frown that I was sure he never had before this weekend, now deep in his brow.

"No. I'm positive. He never once looked in my direction."

"You need to be careful, Aubrey. If Chris saw you tonight, and if he's the killer, that could put you in danger."

"Do we think he is?" I asked.

Ellie opened the notes on her phone. "Our list is quite long, but saving his marriage does give him a good motive."

"And we already established he had means and opportunity," I concluded.

"You need to call Tate and let him know," Spencer warned.

"Yeah... I will."

Ellie noticed my hesitation and tilted her head. "What's that look for? Did something happen with Tate?"

"No, it's just... what do I really have to tell him?"

Spencer leaned forward, his tone serious. "Well, if Chris is involved in Willow's death, Tate needs to know what you overheard tonight."

"I guess so. I'll call him in the morning." The truth was I wasn't looking forward to telling him I'd once again stuck my nose into places he wouldn't like.

"No, you'll call him now while the facts are still bright in your mind," Spencer demanded.

"They don't need to be bright. I have it all recorded." Lifting my phone, I smiled.

"Clever girl," Ellie commented, before standing and stretching. "But Tate will want that as evidence."

My smile dissolved. "I'm not giving him my phone."

"He'll need it long enough to get what he needs off it," Ellie reminded me.

I sighed. "In that case, it's definitely waiting till the morning." As I may or may not have Googled his name earlier today, I needed to remove all traces of my search history before he was getting anywhere near it.

* * *

Detective Galbraith frowned at me. "Now, you stated that you only arrived in Saltwater Bay this morning?"

I nodded.

"You've just inherited this house from Bernice Oldham."

Geez, he'd done his homework quickly.

"Yes, which is why I packed up my life and moved to town."

Detective Galbraith scribbled something in his notepad, then tapped his pen against the page. "Has anyone had access to the house since your grandmother passed?"

"No. It's been locked up. Grayson's been keeping an eye on it for me, but that's it."

"Grayson? The young man who showed you the skull?"

"Uh-huh."

His gaze sharpened. "There was a large storm last night I hear. Are there any signs of disturbance to the property? Broken windows, doors forced? Anything unexpected?"

"Apart from the skull? Not that I can tell. Only the debris under the house."

He nodded again only this time he rhythmically tapped his pen against his palm. "Who has access to that area?"

"Everyone. There're four beach shacks built on the sand like this one. Each has an unmarked boundary. Grayson lives next door, then there's Doris Emmerson, and Joseph McIntyre. Grayson works from home, but the others are retired and only keep them as vacation properties. I have no idea if they're here or away at the moment though."

"Daphne, have you ever met this man?" The detective swiped his phone open and held it toward me, showing a photo of a fifty-something looking man. His hairline was receding, his gold-capped tooth was bucked, and his deep-set eyes were hidden behind thick, rimmed glasses.

"Is that Jenkins Butler?"

"Yes."

"And you believe that's his skull we found?"

"At this stage, it fits. Of course, forensics will do what they do best and will give me a definitive answer. Until then, this murder investigation will center around that." He gave one curt nod of his head.

"Are you sure he was murdered? Couldn't the damage have been done by his remains being washed through cave systems?"

"He was murdered. Preliminary checks show that the injury is not recent."

I gulped.

Detective Galbraith didn't miss a beat. "Is it true that Jenkins Butler and Ms. Oldham had a personal relationship?"

I shook my head as a lump formed in my throat. "I can't answer that as I wasn't privy to Bernie's love life. You'd best ask her friend Maeve Harris. They shared everything."

He sat back in the chair, his gaze once again roaming the room with a mixture of curiosity.

"It's a lovely little house. How long had Ms. Oldham owned it?"

"Umm, about thirty years, I think. After my grandfather passed away, she became very spiritual, and this felt like home. She always said that the ocean and the caves called to her."

"From what I've learned so far, the caves are renowned for being spiritually charged."

"They're pretty special. You should do the tour while you're in town."

"Oh, I intend to. Now," he added, slapping his thighs. "I've held you up long enough. If you remember anything, any little detail, please let me know." He handed me a business card and then once again gave me the kind smile that somehow said he wouldn't miss a thing.

"I'll be sure to let you know."

CHAPTER TEN

Pulled from my fictional world, I blinked against the sting of my eyes. After Ellie and Spencer had gone to bed, my mind wouldn't settle, so I'd used the time to get some words down. Daphne and Grayson and Saltwater Bay certainly soothed any nerves I'd had, and as the words had been flowing, I'd wanted to get them down while I could.

My stiff neck told me it was way past my bedtime, and my back ached from being hunched over my laptop for the last few hours. Yawning, I closed the screen, dropped it onto the bed, and stood, stretching my arms up and enjoying the feeling of relief it gave me.

Despite my body being tired and bruised from my earlier fall, my mind was wired, the potential of Daphne and Grayson humming in my consciousness. I couldn't wait to learn what happened to them, to see what came out on the page as I sat and typed. More often than not it was a surprise to me. Ellie often lectured me on the benefits of plotting my story with detail before sitting down to write it, and as much as I agreed with her, the only things that I ever knew for sure when I started a new book was what my heroine looked like. Of course, I quickly figured out the premise, but my ladies spoke to me, begging me to tell their story. I knew it sounded crazy, but I'd never questioned why it happened this way. And even though reaching the status of Willow Fox wasn't a reality yet, I loved each and every character that I'd written.

I hugged my sweater closer to my body and headed to the kitchen, in need of a piece of the chocolate cake that had been in the fridge last night. The stillness of the mansion unnerved me, and as the wind had picked up outside, every creak and groan the old building made caused me to jump. Clutching my phone like a lifeline, I flipped light switches as I went and found safety in the glow.

Locating the sweet treat I was looking for, I found a fork, then leaned against the counter and took a deep breath, checking Instagram while I dug into the chocolaty goodness.

News of Willow's death filled my feed, with photos of her walking her dog and smiling with her latest paperback in her hand. But the picture of her alongside an unknown woman pushing a stroller was the one that brought a lump to my throat, and I wondered how Willow had felt about being pregnant.

"Hey, Aubrey. I didn't expect you to be awake at this time of night."

I squelched a squeal as I nearly dropped my phone, spinning to see Levi half smiling back at me, his hair whipped from the wind, giving him a crazed look.

"Oh, wow. Sorry. You startled me."

"Didn't mean to. I couldn't sleep, so I decided to go for a walk."

"At midnight? When it's this windy?" I already had a million questions for him, and my mind was whirring at a thousand miles an hour.

"Yeah, well, the energy helps me sort my thoughts. I figured a walk amongst the elements would help."

I nodded despite thinking he was mad. "Did it?"

His smile disappeared as his shoulders dropped, and he shivered, slipping his jacket off and hanging it on a hook by the door. "No. But then why I thought anything would help my grief is beyond me."

Adrenalin settled as I pulled two mugs from the overhead cupboard and moved to the refrigerator for milk. "Grief's a funny creature. We try to block it when really we should take the time to honor it."

"You sound like you know what you're talking about."

My gaze absently dropped to the milk bottle, my memories dancing to my sister Emily and the pain her death had caused. "Yeah. I do."

"Tell me that it will pass, and this ache I have in my chest will cease."

"Sorry. I can't. When I first lost my sister, I too wanted the pain to go away. But as time has gone on, I no longer want it to. I've learned the job of my emotions is to tell me what something means to me, and I never want to forget just how much she was worth." I blinked back tears as her smile filled my mind. "I wish she was still here, and I would give anything to change what happened, but that's not how life works."

Silence sat between us as I stirred cocoa through the milk before putting the cups in the microwave. Once it dinged, I offered one to Levi.

"Life really sucks," he replied, sniffing loudly and accepting my offering as he sat heavily on the nearest chair.

"It sure does. It's unfair and unjust. I've been told the universe has a reason for everything, but I've searched for what possible reason it could justify for taking Emily when it did."

"Did you find one?"

"No. All I found was more questions."

Levi nodded, his thoughts seemingly lost to the steam coming from his cup until he looked up and said, "Everyone thinks Willow didn't love me. That she was with Berkley because he fulfilled her every wish. But they're wrong. She did love me. We had a passion that romance writers fill novels with. We were going to have a family!"

I gasped. So, he was the baby father! "What happened? Why did you break up?"

Levi tensed, anger flashing through his eyes. "Naomi told her that I'd come on to her. That I'd kissed her, and we were having an affair."

"Were you?"

"No! I've never so much as held Naomi's hand." His nostrils flared as his grip on the cup tightened.

"Then why would she say that?"

"Because she's insane. She's in love with me and wouldn't take no for an answer."

Levi wasn't in the same league as Spencer or Tate, but he was pleasant looking. He had a boyish vulnerability about him that I could see Naomi being attracted to. Yet the anger that slipped through the shield when he let his guard down scared me. I'd seen his hands tremble and his muscles tense as he'd looked at Willow, and I could understand why she had a restraining order against him.

Only as he sat here with his heartache did I know just how deeply his love for her went, and I wondered if he was grieving for two lives. After all, there was a possibility Chris was sterile.

"Levi, I don't understand. Why would Willow allow a lie to keep her from the father of her baby?" I know I'd want evidence of the infidelity before I kept him from his child.

His head jerked up to stare at me, and he gasped. "What are you talking about?"

"You just said…" I blinked. "Wait. Didn't you just say you were the father of her baby?"

His eyes narrowed as they stared at me. "There was no baby."

I frowned. "Yes, there was…" I trailed off as my mistake hit me.

"Aubrey, what do you know?" Levi stood abruptly and moved to stand over me.

I shrank back against the counter. "Umm, nothing."

"Aubrey." His tone was low and menacing.

I gulped. "I, I overheard the detective say she was pregnant. I'm sorry. I didn't mean…"

"Pregnant?" His eyes were wide, his breath shallow.

I nodded. "Look, I shouldn't have said anything. Please forget I mentioned it."

His jaw tightened, and his breathing became rapid as he took a large step backwards. "I bet it was Berkley's. That bastard had no right to be with her. He didn't deserve her!" His fist slammed the cupboard door alongside me, and I jumped, slopping cocoa on the floor. "He didn't love her! Not like I did. She would have seen that if she'd given me the time to explain Naomi was a lying, conniving witch! I tried to show her how much I loved her, how I could have given her the life she deserved, but Willow had other plans, didn't she?" Levi spun in a circle, pulling at his hair.

"She always did," he continued, barely taking a breath. "Whatever Willow wanted, she got. And she wanted Berkley. Not because she loved him, but because he could help her career. It was the same with everyone in her life. But if she'd given me the time, I could have shown her that I'm like Berkley. I'm going to write a bestseller. I can be just as great as he is!"

I shrank back as far as I could, one eye on the exit while I monitored his movements.

He turned to me. "Who else knows about this? Who else have you told?"

"No one. Honestly, I've told no one," I lied.

"Good. Then I suggest you don't."

I nodded rapidly.

"Keep it that way." With that, he turned abruptly and stormed from the room. Only when I heard his footsteps on the stairs did I sink onto the nearest chair and take some slow calming breaths.

I had no idea how long I sat there trying to stop the shaking that seemed to have taken hold of me. When my legs no longer threatened to give out, I stood, longing for a hot shower and bed. Tomorrow was our last day at the retreat, and I'd never wished to go home more than I did now.

But thinking over Levi's reaction definitely filled me with questions. Could he have killed Willow in a fit of jealousy? He had the anger to do it. He genuinely seemed shocked by the news that she was pregnant. Would he have taken her back if he knew she was pregnant with another man's baby? Or was he pretending he didn't know to cover for the fact he killed her once he'd learned the news?

Emptying the last of my cocoa into the sink, I made my way to my room, allowing theories to run rampant in my mind. I had a list of suspects, and a ton of motives, but were any of them enough to kill over? *Urgh!* How did Tate do this for a living?

As I walked, I one-handed typed a message to both Spencer and Ellie, telling them about Levi and knowing they would get it in the morning when they woke up.

I'd just hit send when I reached my room. Tucking my phone under my arm, I used my key to unlock my door. Yawning, I flipped the light switch up and kicked off my shoes before making my way to the shower, pushing the bathroom door closed behind me with my foot.

I hadn't realized how tired I was until the hot water pummeled my skin. I thought retreats were supposed to be relaxing. But then I'd never imagined this one would turn out the way it had.

Closing my eyes, I leaned against the tiled porcelain wall and allowed my mind to wander over the situation.

I tried to meditate, allowing my subconscious to show me what I couldn't see. Only before long, I was dreaming of Emily waving goodbye to me. Her smile was bright as she was filled with excitement for the night she was about to have with her friends. She'd asked me to join her, but I'd been tired, so I'd declined. If only I'd known that was a decision I'd live to regret. After all, if I'd been with her, maybe I would have been driving. I could have saved her.

It wasn't the first time I'd drifted into a light sleep while standing, but it was the slipping against the tiles and knocking my head that woke me.

Blinking rapidly against my tears, I turned the taps off and reached for my towel. In my hurry to get in the shower, I'd left my pajamas on the bed, so I wrapped the towel tight around me and made my way to the bedroom. Pushing the door open, I stepped into the darkness. Hmmm, that was weird as I knew I'd left the light on.

Looking for the lamp switch, a shadow crossed my path. I halted, my hand flew to my chest, and I gasped.

Standing in front of me was a hooded figure, the light spilling from the bathroom glinting against the headless bronzed statue they held raised above me.

I screamed as it came down hard against my head. The sound of breathing echoed in my ears as pain shot through my skull, and the world turned to black.

* * *

"Aubrey! Aubrey, can you hear me?"

I fluttered my eyelashes as Spencer's blue eyes scanned my body, concern etched into the creases at their corners.

I groaned and attempted to sit up, but my head pounded, and nausea swirled.

"What... what happened?" I asked as his strong arms cocooned me in a feeling of safety.

"Geez, I thought you were dead."

The thumping inside my skull definitely told me I was alive. I lifted my hand to my temple. A trickle of warm blood intermingled with my fingers, and the world spun a little bit more.

"*Urgh,*" I moaned, fighting the urge to gag. I hated blood. And when it was my own, I hated it even more.

"It's okay," Spencer whispered, his voice shaky. "I've called the paramedics. Help is on the way." His hand trembled as his grip on my shoulders tightened.

Pain shot through my retinas from the light overhead. I hurriedly slammed my eyelids shut and took a moment, enjoying Spencer's warmth before I attempted to put everything together. I mean, how did I end up on the floor with Spencer holding me in a death grip? And hang on! Am I only wearing a towel?

"Aubrey! Aubrey!" Footsteps thundered into the room, along with Ellie's voice impersonating Minnie Mouse.

I groaned and sat up, leaning against Spencer for support, gripping the edges of the towel and hoping I hadn't embarrassed myself by giving him a viewing of my lady garden. But at least it was pruned.

"Oh thank goodness. You're alive." Ellie stopped next to Spencer and punched him on the shoulder.

"Ow. What was that for?"

"Your message said you'd found Aubrey lying on the floor, blood all over her, barely breathing! You scared the heck out of me!" Her eyes were wide, her breath ragged.

"I'm sorry for scaring you, but that's not what my message said."

Ellie scoffed and pulled her phone from her pocket. Tapping at the screen, she stopped and read, "Ellie, just found Aubrey lying on the floor in her room. Looks like someone has hit her. She's bleeding, and I've called the paramedics. Can you let them in when they get here, please." She lowered the phone and glared at Spencer. "See what I mean?"

"No, I don't. My message was clear and concise. At no point did I say Aubrey was barely breathing."

"Guys," I managed. "Keep it down, please. I kind of feel a bit sick."

"Are you going to vomit?" Ellie asked, wildly looking around her.

"No." Maybe.

"Where are your clothes?" she asked as I self-consciously crossed my arms over my chest.

"Ellie, I can hear sirens." Spencer either hadn't noticed my attire, or he was a gentleman and chose not to comment on it. "The paramedics must be here. Can you go and let them in like I asked you to, please?"

"No. As soon as I got your message, I threw my pajamas on and called Isla. She's getting Chris to let them in."

Spencer sighed, and footsteps thundered on the floors below us.

"Aubrey, what happened?" Ellie asked, crouching in front of me as we waited for the paramedics to reach us.

Leaning against Spencer, I allowed my thoughts to scramble into place.

"Someone was in my room. I think it was Levi." Or Chris? Did Ricky see me hiding behind the wall? Or could it have been Naomi?

"Levi hit you?" Spencer tensed.

"I... I don't know for sure." A lone tear trickled down my cheek, and I started to shake. "I really didn't see who it was."

"What did you see?" Spencer questioned. Only I didn't get a chance to answer him as two paramedics pushed their way into the now crowded room.

Expertly assessing my condition, they soon declared I could be moved, and I was helped to the bed, where the soft mattress felt like heaven.

I'd gathered quite a crowd outside my door. But then as the guests were all authors with very vivid imaginations, I figured the arrival of paramedics in the early hours of the morning would rouse curiosity. I prickled when I saw Chris, but he was now telling people to go back to bed as Isla looked more than slightly annoyed. Ellie and Spencer stood against the wall, allowing the medics to do their thing.

"Am I going to live?" I asked the one who looked like he'd seen more than his share of emergencies.

"It seems that way." His crooked grin filled me with comfort. "But you do have quite a bump growing there. I'd like you to go to the hospital and get it scanned."

I didn't like the idea of what that would do to my insurance premium.

I shook my head. "No. I'm fine. Honestly. The nausea has even settled."

"You can't be too careful with head injuries."

"You should follow his recommendations." A deep, familiar voice sounded from behind. I glanced over my shoulder to see Tate striding in. He'd changed since earlier in the evening, now wearing sweatpants and a zip up hoodie. His eyes were bloodshot, and I figured he'd been woken from sleep.

"What are you doing here?" I asked, surprised to see him.

"I got a call from the station that there had been an attack here tonight. As soon as they mentioned your name, I got here as quickly as I could. I wondered if you were sticking your nose into my investigation again," Tate finished, his lips in a tight line.

The paramedic's grin kicked up a notch as he closed his bag of medical goodies and stepped back to allow Tate in close. As Tate had his notebook already in his hand, I figured this wasn't a courtesy call. Only as his gaze roamed over my towel clad body before landing on the Band-Aid now stuck to my forehead, his frown softened, and he gave me a weak smile.

Heat traveled up my neck, and now more than ever I wished I'd taken my pj's into the bathroom. At least that way, I wouldn't be sitting in front of all and sundry in not much more than my birthday suit. These towels were sumptuous, but they sure weren't thick enough for the occasion.

"Care to tell me what happened?" Tate asked.

Not really.

"That's if you're up to it," he finished.

I reluctantly told him what I could recall from the attack. By the time that I'd finished, his frown was once again cemented on his brow, and the smile had disappeared.

"Spencer, why were you the one to find Aubrey?" Tate challenged.

Spencer jolted. "I woke up to her message about Levi and wanted to see if she was okay. I called, but when she didn't answer I went to her bedroom door. Only before I got there, I heard her scream, so I ran up to see what had happened." He looked at me, and his eyes softened. "I think my heart stopped when I saw you lying on the floor, bleeding."

"Did you see anyone leaving the room? In the hallway?"

Spencer shook his head. "No. I was more worried about helping Aubrey."

Tate took a slow, deep breath before turning back to me.

"So you didn't see who hit you?" he confirmed.

"No. Only a hooded figure."

"Were they tall? Short?"

"Taller than me."

"Most people are taller than you," Ellie called, moving past Chris and stopping alongside Tate.

I huffed. "It felt like they were male. Or female."

"Felt like?" Spencer queried.

"How so?" Tate asked.

"I don't really know," I admitted. "It could have been Levi because I'd just questioned him about Willow being pregnant."

Isla gasped. Oh geez. I'd forgotten she was there. "What?" she demanded. "How does she know about that?"

Tate pinched the bridge of his nose, his eyes momentarily closing.

"It was in the autopsy," he declared quietly.

Thankfully, Chris had managed to get Nancy and Beverley back to their rooms, or that news could have been spread across the state before daybreak.

"Why haven't we been informed of this?" Anger flashed in Isla's eyes. "What else did the autopsy show?"

"I'm very sorry, Mrs. Woods," Tate soothed. "It was a call that Aubrey inadvertently overheard earlier this evening. I had every intention of speaking to you in the morning about it." He shot me a death stare.

"That's completely inappropriate! What kind of a detective are you who allows strangers privy to that kind of information?"

"Like I said, I'm very sorry. I will speak to you in private about this, but considering the time is now two a.m., I suggest you go back to bed, and we'll reconvene after breakfast."

Isla's face reddened as her gaze bounced from Tate to me and back again. Her hand movements were jerky as Chris glared at me before taking her arm.

"Come on," he said. "I'll get you a drink. It'll help calm your nerves."

I didn't know what unsettled me more—Chris being so calm or Isla being so agitated. Either way, neither of them were looking overly surprised to see me with the paramedics.

"Don't tell me what to do," she snapped, snatching her arm from his grasp. However, she did stomp toward her room. As a door slammed, heavy footsteps faded down the stairs. If Isla's mood was anything to go by, I figured Chris would be looking for a spare bed.

Tate watched them go, his eyes sharp and seemingly taking in every detail.

"If you don't want to go to the hospital," the paramedic interrupted my thoughts, "then we'll leave you to it. I suggest you put some ice on the bump you have, take some Tylenol for the headache, and rest. No screens and no sports for forty-eight hours. And someone should check on you regularly tonight. If anything changes, or your symptoms get worse, please call us or get someone to take you straight to the hospital." He looked around our group, and we all nodded. Seemingly satisfied I'd behave or at least have someone watch over me, he nodded to his partner, and they headed out after Chris.

That left Tate, Ellie, and Spencer all staring at me, their expressions grim.

I'd disappointed them, each of them worried in a different way.

"I am really sorry," I said as tears stung my eyes. "I never meant to upset you."

"Aubrey, do you remember the warning I gave only a few hours ago?" Tate's voice was barely above a whisper, his jaw tense.

"The one where you said there was a murderer running around?" I swiped at a tear as it escaped, more upset with myself than they were.

"I meant it when I said I don't want to investigate your death. And I'm sure your friends don't want to witness it either."

"So, now's not a good time to tell you about my evening?" I gulped but knew I had to come clean.

When I finished retelling my tale about Chris, Spencer had his hands jammed under his arms and a muscle ticked in his jaw, and tears brimmed Ellie's lashes.

"What do I have to do for you to take me seriously?" Tate asked.

One hand gripped the towel as I threw the other one up in surrender, and I replied, "I'm sorry about following Chris. It was stupid, but may I remind you that I was stepping out of the shower in my own private room when I was attacked!"

"I understand that. But if you'd been minding your own business, like I told you to, maybe it wouldn't have happened. And did you lock the door after you entered your room?"

I thought I had.

"For what it's worth, I don't think my attacker wanted to kill me. It felt more like a warning shot."

"What makes you so sure of that?" Tate challenged.

"Because if it was the murderer who hit me, they've already shown they are capable of killing when needed. If they wanted me dead, then I'd be dead."

Ellie suppressed a cry, Spencer groaned, and Tate exhaled very loudly.

"Look," I hurriedly added. "The point I'm trying to make is that whoever hit me didn't want me dead."

"And that's supposed to make us feel better?" Spencer yelled.

"Well, I'm not particularly fond of the idea that someone was in my room either." Tears welled again as the weight of the situation sat heavy on my heart. I wanted to put on a brave face so my friends wouldn't worry, but the truth was I was more than a little freaked out.

"I'll stay with you tonight, Aubrey," Ellie said, moving in to give me a hug. "And I'll double-check the door is locked."

I nodded and blinked the tears back. "Thank you."

That seemed to satisfy the men for now. Once everyone had left, I swapped the towel for pj's, Ellie pushed a chair under the door handle, flipped the light off, and then settled in beside me.

"I really am okay," I mumbled as she tucked the blanket around my shoulders.

"Sure. But you're not getting cold on my watch."

I smiled into the darkness despite feeling like a child.

"Hey, Aubrey. What was Spencer really doing in your room?"

"What do you mean? He said he was responding to the message I sent."

"That could have waited until the morning. Do you know what I think?"

"I'm sure you're going to tell me."

The sheets rustled as Ellie rolled toward me. "I think he came to see you. Romantically." Her sigh was blissful.

"Are you sure you're not the one who got hit on the head?"

"Come on! It was the early hours of the morning, and he's heading to your room to talk to you about Levi?" The insinuation was heavy in her words, and for a delicious moment, I indulged her theory.

"He doesn't like me that way." I attempted to push down the hope her words gave me.

"Of course, he does," she said matter-of-factly. "You can tell by the way he tenses whenever Tate's near you."

"I don't know why he would."

"Why he'd like you?" Ellie sounded puzzled. "Or why he tenses when Tate's around?"

"Either."

"Aubrey, everyone can see the way Tate looks at you."

I sat up and leaned against the pillow, intrigued. "How does he look at me?"

"Like you're a lost kitty cat that needs his care." I heard the smile in her voice.

"*Hmph*. I don't want to be a lost kitty." I flopped back onto the pillow and stared into the darkness.

"What do you want to be?"

"Wonder Woman."

Ellie laughed. "I love you, my friend, but you're definitely not Wonder Woman. You're more like a blonde Sandra Bullock in *Miss Congeniality*."

"Before or after her makeover?"

"After of course!"

"I can live with that."

We lay in silence as I considered the possibility that Spencer was bothered by another man, and before long, Ellie's breathing slowed into a gentle rhythm.

As she slept soundly beside me, her gentle breathing only broken by the occasional word as she spoke in her sleep, I groaned. It seemed that, despite the possibility of a concussion, sleep wasn't on my radar. But then that could have been because I'd never been able to sleep with a headache.

Fumbling on the bedside table in the dark for my phone, I clicked the button and allowed the light from the screen to guide my way toward the Tylenol I'd yet to take. However, that wouldn't go down without water, and as my glass was now empty, I knew that sleep would have to wait until I'd rectified it.

Careful not to disturb Ellie, I pulled the blanket back and swung my legs over the edge of the bed, clutching my phone tightly as I tiptoed toward the bathroom. Only before I got there, a loud *thump* outside my bedroom door, followed by low-level cursing, made me stop.

I froze, straining to hear what was going on, my heart pounding just a little bit harder.

Someone was out there. Were they coming back to finish me off?

"Ellie! Ellie," I hissed, not wanting to be too loud. "Wake up."

She stirred but only rolled over in her sleep, pulling the pillow over her head.

Well, she wasn't going to be any help.

Tentatively, I crept toward the door and placed my ear against the wood, straining to listen. A floorboard creaked outside the door before footsteps slowly moved away.

I sucked in a deep breath, as quietly as possible unlocked the latch, and pulled the door open an inch, wanting to see who was out there. Chris had turned off the overhead lights, and only the night lights lined the hall. That was fine by me as any light seemed to be enhancing my headache.

It didn't, however, show me who was there.

I held my breath, wanting to know who'd been sneaking around but not quite brave enough to venture into the semidarkness, so instead, I aimed the camera on my phone into the hall and hit click. The flash immediately illuminated the area, and I heard the gasp before I could check the screen to see what I'd captured.

Immediately closing the door, I checked the grainy image, but even with the low resolution, I could clearly make out Naomi, her suitcase in her hand, creeping toward the stairs.

Why was she sneaking out at this time of the morning? Was she guilty and wanting to escape before Tate could arrest her?

Before she could get too far, I made a fast decision, grabbed the bottle of perfume I'd left on the bedside table, and opened the bedroom door. The perfume may not be a great weapon, but a good shot to the eyes and she'd be crying for weeks.

"Ellie!" I hissed. "Wake up. I need back up!"

Ellie stirred behind me and moved the pillow from her face. Only I couldn't wait any longer, as Naomi was getting away and I wanted to know what she was up to.

Hurriedly entering the hallway, I kept to the shadows and followed Naomi's footsteps echoing down the stairs. Seconds later, the front door lock clunked, and I made another fast decision to follow her. Only guilty people ran like that in the middle of the night.

Tate's warning sang in harmony with the pounding behind my eyes. But then I had no intention of chasing her down. No, I only needed to follow her. Stay in the shadows and see what she was doing. Plus, Ellie had already been stirring when I left, so I knew she wouldn't be far behind me.

Naomi flung the door open and hurled herself into the outside darkness, and I forced my feet to move. Reaching the door, I blinked, willing my eyes to adjust, but whether the headache was contributing or I was just plain tired, my eyes weren't up to the job, and within seconds, Naomi disappeared into the night.

She was acting very suspicious, and I couldn't let her get away, so I picked up my pace and hit dial on my phone, calling Tate so he could get back here and arrest her. For what exactly? Killing Willow? Attacking me? Well, I'd leave that up to Tate to figure out.

The ringing was loud in my ear as I willed the phone to connect. Finally Tate's weary voice answered, and I breathlessly explained to him what was happening.

"You're still here, right?" I asked him hopefully.

"No. I'm almost at the station."

"Then you need to turn around. Fast! Naomi's getting away."

"Aubrey, what are you talking about?"

"Naomi. She's leaving."

"Are you running after her?" His tone was incredulous.

"Yes! She's bypassed the parking lot and is heading toward the orchard. Maybe she's secretively meeting an accomplice. Maybe she's stashed a vehicle that can't be traced to her. I honestly have no idea why she's acting like this, but it's not normal!" My patience was running thin. "Just hurry… up… and… get here." I fought to catch my breath as I picked up speed. I wasn't cut out for this. In fact, did I really care if she got away? Surely, Tate could track her down and arrest her from wherever she went?

I ended the call, and my steps slowed as I reached a red brick path winding its way toward the Victorian greenhouse. The path lighting sparkled in the frost on the skeletal remains of a rose garden, condensation shimmering on the glass. I was about to switch on my torch when the floodlights on the glass greenhouse flashed to life, filling the gardens with light. Naomi turned, her mouth fell open as she stared back at me, and then she stumbled on a rock, dropping the handle on her suitcase.

Her arms flapped about her head as she struggled to keep her balance, and I saw my opportunity. I sucked in a deep breath, turned up the throttle, and powered toward her. As she attempted to regain her footing, I took the chance and launched myself, my body pummeling into hers and knocking us both to the ground.

Urgh! That wasn't as graceful as I'd hoped it would be.

Naomi groaned.

I took a moment before rolling off her and nearly threw up.

"What the heck is wrong with you?" she demanded, lying flat on her back, defeat oozing from her every pore.

Sitting up on the damp grass, I took a few slow deep breaths.

"Me? You're the one skulking out at an ungodly hour!" Keeping my head between my knees I willed the world to stop spinning. Where the heck was Ellie when I needed her?

"I wasn't skulking!"

"Then why did you run when you saw me?" Against my better judgment, I lifted my head as I demanded answers.

"Because I thought you wanted to attack me!" Her eyes bulged as her mouth hung open. "You were taking sneaky photos of me!"

"What? No I wasn't!" I sat up straight, ready to defend myself. "Okay, I was, but it's not like that. I'm not a creepy stalker or anything."

"No. You're a murderer who was going to kill me too." Naomi pushed up on her knees and stood, a rock held tightly in her hand. "I've got a weapon. I will defend myself."

My head shot up to look at her, and I had to hold the ground for support. "Wait a second. I'm not going to attack you. I'm not a murderer! What possible motive would I have for killing Willow? Or you for that matter?"

Naomi sneered as she wiped some damp grass from her jeans. "You were jealous of her fame."

I sucked in a fast, indignant breath.

"Don't you turn this on me. You were in my room tonight, and you hit me to stop me from telling the truth." I had no idea what I was doing, so making it up as I went along seemed like the best thing to do.

Even under the stark floodlights, the color drained from her cheeks.

"What truth?" she challenged. "I wasn't in your room!"

"But you were in Willow's last night."

Her shoulders drooped as the life seemed to fade out of her. Thankfully, she dropped the rock.

"What makes you think anyone was in there?" she asked.

"I heard you."

"You can't prove I broke in."

"No, but I bet Tate can. And he's on his way. I called him." I grinned, extremely happy with myself for my quick thinking.

"Seriously? You think *I* killed Willow? Why would I do that?"

"Because you love Levi. And he loved Willow. You were the jealous one."

She planted her hands on her hips and scoffed.

"If I'm wrong, why are you running?" I asked.

"I had an argument with Ricky. I punched him, and he threatened to call the police. When I saw them turn up, I figured they were looking for me, so I hid out until they were gone. I've had enough of all the drama that surrounds Willow, so I'm moving to California to be near my mom."

Oh, well that wasn't the answer I'd been looking for. "What happened between you and Ricky?"

"He's an arrogant ass who tried to blackmail me."

Sounded like that was his full-time occupation.

"Why would he do that?" I asked.

Fatigue settled on Naomi's shoulders, and she sank onto the grass alongside me, completely deflated. "Because I borrowed some of Willow's money. He found out about it and was going to tell Willow. It's why he was here."

"I'm assuming she didn't know you borrowed it."

"No. But I had every intention of paying it back. I only needed one big win, and all my troubles would be over."

I raised an eyebrow, considering her words.

"I love the ponies," she confessed. "But lately I haven't been picking the winners very well. I was behind on my rent, Willow often paid my salary late, and I was getting desperate. And you have no idea how much work I did for that woman! I considered it more of a wage adjustment." Naomi shrugged.

"How did Ricky know about it?"

Naomi's sigh came straight from her soul. "Pillow talk. I made the mistake of telling him way too much, about things I should never have mentioned. I thought I could trust him, but it turns out he's a dirty lying scumbag."

I grimaced, almost feeling sorry for her.

"That's why you didn't want him to be a part of the weekend."

"Yeah. I told Jenna that it was Willow, but it was me that refused his ticket."

"Did Willow find out, and that's why she was going to fire you?"

Naomi gulped. "You really are nosy, aren't you?"

"I'm inquisitive. And I don't stop until I've learnt the truth. You killed Willow."

"No! I didn't kill her! I was with Ricky at the time. I saw Jenna remove him from the dining room, and I knew why he was there. I followed him out to the pond, and we were negotiating terms when Willow died. You can ask him."

"But why did he tell Spencer he wanted to speak to Willow about a book?"

Naomi shrugged. "Ricky has a lot of side hustles going on. Who knows what he was up to."

My own shoulders sank. Just when I thought I had it, turns out I was wrong. I couldn't solve a thing.

"Don't beat yourself up," Naomi offered kindly. "My money's on Isla."

"The whole Chris and Willow having an affair thing?" Naomi grinned. "You're better at this than you think."

"How did you know about the affair?"

"I caught them in the act one day." Naomi grimaced.

"That's why you were blackmailing him."

She at least had the decency to look sheepish about it. "Yeah, not my finest behavior, but he owed me for not divulging his dirty little secrets." She shrugged.

A few pieces of the puzzle were clicking together. "Do you think Isla knew about the affair? Would she kill her own sister if she did?"

"When she found out Willow was pregnant, she would have been furious. Especially if there's a chance Chris could be the father." Naomi looked into the distance, her thoughts unreadable.

"But she only learned about the pregnancy tonight when I spilled the beans."

Naomi shook her head. "No, she didn't. The doctor sent a specialist referral for Willow to see an obstetrician, but he sent it to the wrong email address. Isla was there when I opened it on Friday."

So that's how Ricky knew about the baby. Naomi really had trusted the wrong person.

"Chris and Isla have been trying to get pregnant for years," Naomi continued. "They've done the whole IVF thing, but nothing's worked. I overheard Willow and Isla talking about it one day. But if he'd gotten Willow pregnant after all that, Isla would have seen red. If I were you, I'd be asking Isla her whereabouts at the time of the murder."

Footfalls on the path startled me, and I looked up into the stony face of Detective Tate.

"She'll do no such thing," he stated in no uncertain terms.

* * *

"So let me get this straight." Spencer dropped his spoon into his cereal bowl and leaned his elbows on the dining table, staring hard at me. "After we left you in bed, you chased down

Naomi? Knocking her to the ground and getting a confession that she stole money from Willow."

"Uh-huh. And she said I need to ask Isla where she was at the time of the murder," I finished, inhaling the rich aroma of coffee. My head pounded despite the amount of Tylenol I'd consumed, and I was hoping the caffeine would help. "And I need to do that in the next two hours before we leave." A heavy sigh escaped my lips. "I have a new respect for detectives. This investigation bit is really hard."

"And dangerous," Spencer added. "What you did was stupid, Aubrey! What if Naomi had been the killer? If she'd killed over blackmail, she most certainly would have killed to stop the truth of her being a murderer being leaked."

"I didn't intend to catch up with her. I only wanted to follow her until Tate got there. I wasn't going to tackle her."

"But you did." Spencer's eyes flashed with anger as he sat back in his chair and glared at me.

"Don't be so hard on her, Spence." Ellie rubbed my arm sympathetically. "Tate took Naomi in for questioning over the theft, so all's well that ends well."

"But it very nearly didn't end well!" Spencer threw his arms in the air and bumped the back of Nancy's head in the process. He immediately turned to her. "I'm so sorry, Nancy. Are you okay? Did I hurt you?" Genuine concern burned bright in his eyes.

"I'm fine, Spencer. Don't worry about me. But these chairs are very close together this morning. Looks like housekeeping needs to have a talking to." Dismissing him, she turned back to the notes she was scribbling in her book.

Spencer scraped his chair as close to our table as he could before picking the conversation back up right where he'd left it.

"And where were you when all this was happening to Aubrey?" he challenged Ellie. "You were supposed to be watching her!"

Ellie flinched, her gaze darted from Spencer to me, and her eyes filled. Turns out Ellie hadn't heard me calling her and had slept through the entire event.

"Don't blame her," I cut in before she could beat herself up. "It was all me. And I'm sorry. It wasn't my finest moment."

"Please tell me that you'll leave this alone now?" Spencer pleaded.

"You sound like Tate," I whined, taking a large sip of hot coffee.

"Maybe it's one thing we can agree on then." Spencer scoffed.

"Why do you dislike him so much?" I asked.

"I don't dislike him. I just think he's not as good a detective as he thinks he is." Spencer leaned close again. "Did you know he was relocated here after an undercover investigation went wrong in New York? He moved here for his own safety."

I gulped. "How do you know that?"

"Research for my novels has led to a friendship with a detective in the Seattle PD. I spoke to him about Tate."

"That would have been really tough for Tate," Ellie said.

"Ellie, he botched the job. A killer was set free because he didn't follow protocol. I'm not feeling sorry for him."

"Well, as long as he doesn't botch this investigation, it's none of our business," Ellie stated, pushing a piece of bacon onto her fork. "Now, Aubrey, do we believe what Naomi told you?"

"I have no reason not to," I replied, yet my mind was whirling with Spencer's announcement.

"You need to invite Tate for coffee and see if you can find out what this case is up to," she pressed.

"Umm, I'm not so sure he'll be that chatty. He was pretty uptight with me when he left last night."

"Maybe he's not so stupid after all." Spencer scowled, and I figured any chance I may have had at romance were dwindling fast this weekend.

"We'll stop at the bakery on the way to the police station this afternoon," Ellie announced. "Tate's weak spot is apple Danish."

"How on earth do you know that?"

"I'm married, Aubrey. You learn to notice the little things."

I shrugged, wondering if I'd be single forever because I certainly hadn't noticed Tate's appreciation for baked goods.

"When we get to the station, what are we going to do?" I asked, wanting to drown my sorrows in caffeine.

"*We're* not going to do anything. I'm waiting in the car while you go and flutter those long lashes at him. He'll tell you anything you want then."

Spencer gave a disgusted grunt before standing and stomping off to the buffet table.

"You know none of this explains the ripped page from the notebook," I mused, stirring an extra sugar into my coffee.

"Maybe it's not important."

"Hmm, maybe. But it's a loose end, and I hate loose ends."

"This could help. I made it to thank Jenna and Isla." Ellie pulled a large card from her bag and handed it to me. The cover was handmade with a sketched book surrounded by lots of swirly hearts and the words *Thank You* written in beautiful scroll. "The weekend turned so awful I thought it might cheer them up. And it can serve two purposes as I never got around to getting handwriting samples to compare to the page." She grinned. "What I need you to do is get everyone to sign it."

"Really? Why can't you do it? I just want to sit here and inhale the scent of baked goods."

"I've got to call Joel and tell him what time to expect me home, and Spencer's already gone. Sorry my friend, but the task is yours."

I sighed and accepted the job.

* * *

After Ellie had left, I stared out the window and admired the view one last time, nibbling on a croissant. I was going to miss the buffet breakfast once I went home, but as much as I wanted to indulge, my stomach wasn't settled.

"Good morning, Aubrey," Beverley almost sang as she placed a plate of bacon and eggs on a table opposite mine. "Can you believe it's our last day here? The weekend went so quickly."

"It definitely didn't turn out the way I was expecting," I added, turning to face her and noting her long green poncho covering her red jeans.

She sighed. "No, but we have to look at the bright side. We got to watch a real-life investigation take place."

"Shame we didn't learn who killed Willow though."

"I'm sure it will turn up on social media one day. Oh, what's that?" she asked, nodding to the card that Ellie had made.

"It's for Jenna and Isla. Would you mind signing it? You can write whatever you want," I added, handing it to her along with a pen Ellie had left.

"I hate being the first to write in a card," she commented. "It's so much easier once you know what others are going to say." I silently agreed with her as she opened it and scribbled some words.

"I'm sure Jenna and Isla will be grateful for whatever you've written." As she handed it back, I checked the writing and ruled her out as being the author of the ripped page.

"You haven't seen Jonathan Berkley around, have you?" I asked. He still seemed to be mysteriously hiding out somewhere in the hotel. I kind of wished I'd met him. Despite thinking he could still be a suspect, the idea of meeting an author as famous as he was thrilled me.

"No. Kara told me that she saw him looking over the lake yesterday morning, but when she got outside to chat to him, he'd gone."

"Why do you think he hasn't interacted with us?"

"Well, Aubrey, he's a very famous man. I believe his visit here was personal and not part of the retreat. With what happened, I can understand him not wanting to socialize."

I guessed she was correct. I picked up the card as I spotted Nancy now sitting at a table nearest the buffet.

"Excuse me, Beverley. I need to get some signatures."

My sneakers squeaked on the wood flooring as I moved across the room.

"Hi, Nancy." I sat on the dining chair opposite her and placed the card on the table. She glanced up from her bowl of porridge, her irritation etched into her brow. "Sorry to interrupt, but we're putting a card together for Jenna and Isla. Would you like to sign it?"

Her mood settled. "Of course. Isla seems like a lovely lady. It's so very sad what's happened." Nancy's chin quivered as she dropped her spoon and took the card. Only just as she started to write her condolences, Kara approached and sat heavily on the round table, causing it to topple. Nancy squealed and grabbed her coffee cup before it could spill, and I grabbed the card and hugged it to my chest, knowing the effort that Ellie had put into it and not wanting to be the one to tell her it had been destroyed in my care.

"You look… astounding," I commented, staring at Kara. Today her skin-tight jeans were accompanied by hooker heels, and her half unbuttoned white blouse displayed her ample assets. As I was almost eye level with them, I wasn't quite sure where to look.

"Thanks. Heading home to hubby, and I don't want his eye wandering. You have to put in the effort, Aubrey." As she spoke, her gaze flipped over my body. As I'd only dressed in gray sweatpants, white T-shirt, and my black hoodie, I guessed there was a reason I was single. But hey, I was happy that I'd managed to brush my hair this morning.

"Ellie told me to come in here and sign a card?" she continued as she smacked her painted lips together.

"Oh, yes. Of course." To be honest, I felt like a teenage boy, barely able to pull my gaze away from her chest. As a woman who'd inherited her mother's double A cup, envy stabbed at my heart.

Kara took the card and with a flourishing script wrote her condolences to Isla. She finished it with large *X*'s and *O*'s.

"I think we have to meet Isla in the library in about an hour," she said, handing it back to me. "Gives me enough time for a cup of coffee and then duck upstairs to pack. What about you, Nancy? Want to share one more cinnamon roll with me?"

"No, thank you. I might go and finish my packing now." Her hand shook as she held her cup to her lips and swallowed hard.

* * *

When I'd arrived at the Grand Hotel Friday afternoon, I'd thought it was a place that I would come back to. After all, it was only twenty minutes from my houseboat, and now that it was open to the public, I imagined bringing my laptop here and writing my latest work. But after the events that had occurred, I didn't ever want to return. Which is why I thought I would get to the library early and get the last words on the page before it was time to go home.

A large plush velvet chair by the window was vacant, so I sank into it and sighed.

"Aubrey!"

I jumped so high my backside lifted off the chair.

"We don't start for another half an hour." Isla stood ramrod straight alongside the bookcase in the far corner, her brown sweater blending with the wood.

"Oh! You scared me. I didn't see you there." A palpitation hit hard in my chest, and I wondered if I should restart the Zoloft the doctor had prescribed me last year.

"I was setting the room up for our last meeting."

"Am I disturbing you?"

She huffed. "I suppose not."

I nodded and pulled my laptop from my tote.

Isla looked past me toward the window, and for a moment, her gaze drifted into the unknown. Deep crevices were etched into her brow, and her eyes glistened. She didn't look like a woman who'd just killed her sister. In fact, I recognized that look. She was a woman grieving.

"Are you okay?"

She stiffened. "Of course."

"It's been such an awful weekend—"

"I'm sorry it turned out so horribly," she cut me off. "Please know I will refund your money in full."

"Don't worry about that. I know it will all get sorted. But I am curious. Why did you keep the retreat running after Willow died? I know when I found out about Emily I could barely get out of bed for a week."

"Not all families are close."

"It seemed like you were close. After all, didn't Willow purchase this hotel for you?"

"Don't be fooled by appearances. They can be very deceiving."

I nodded, momentarily lost in thought about Willow. "Relationships can be tricky. I was lucky to get the family I have. I'd do whatever I needed to protect it."

Isla snapped her head around to glare at me. "What exactly do you mean by that?"

"Just that if someone was trying to take them away from me, I'd do whatever I could to stop them." A cheating husband? Maybe not so much.

Isla took a controlled breath. "Well, it sounds like your family is just as lucky to have you. I hope they appreciate that."

"I know Emily did. She was my big sister and would have protected me any way she could."

Isla turned her face downward, her gaze lost to a memory. Words played on her lips, and I gave her the space to say what was on her mind.

"As children, Jane and I were very close."

"Jane?"

"Willow's real name. Jane Jamison. Not quite as fancy as Willow Fox, is it?" A wry smile twisted her lips.

"I guess she had a part to play. I'm sure being famous isn't all easy."

Isla gave a bark of laughter. "She loved every moment of the spotlight being on her. And she played the part to the max. Fame, fortune, and money. She always wanted it all. But I never thought she would take everything she wanted from me. I never thought she'd take…"

The air stilled as I held my breath. I knew she was referring to Chris, but I wanted her to say the words.

Isla gulped hard before lifting her gaze to meet mine. "You're not married, are you?"

I shook my head as a weight shifted near my heart.

"Keep it that way. Never trust anyone. Not fully. Because when you do, you give them the power to take your entire life from you."

"Is that what Willow did? She took Chris from you?" I wasn't sure what would hurt the most. Your husband betraying you that way, or your sister betraying you that way.

Tears welled in Isla's eyes. "I guess I wasn't the sister he really wanted."

"You don't think she held the guilt in that?"

Isla threw her head back and laughed. "I told you, Willow took whatever she wanted. Everyone thought she was this warmhearted, loving woman. Oh, she was all of that. But only to those that could give her what she needed. Only those who could push her along the path to fame."

"Then why did she go for Chris?" Confusion pinched my brow.

"To hurt me of course!"

"But why would she want to hurt you?" The sibling rivalry she described was beyond anything I could understand.

"Because she was spiteful." Isla's voice was tight with resentment. "And when I had an offer to publish a book I'd written, it threatened her. She wouldn't be the center of attention in the family anymore. So, she took the one thing I had that she didn't—my husband. My chance at a family."

"And that made you angry." Butterflies danced in my belly. Was she about to confess to murder?

"Of course, it made me angry! But before you go accusing me of pushing her out of the window, think again. As much as I hated her, I hate Chris more." Her hand shook as she swiped at the tears that tumbled off her chin. "He's the one I want to kill! He was supposed to be my soulmate. The one person in this world who always had my back. It was in his marriage vows! Do you know what that feels like, Aubrey? To be betrayed by the one person who vowed to always be there for you. For better or worse. Sure, we'd had our struggles, but I thought we were stronger than that." She blew a breath between her teeth as tears tumbled over her cheeks. She angrily swiped at them. "What an idiot I am."

"You're not an idiot to have faith in someone. To have trusted him. What he did was wrong. But what Willow did was worse!" Anger for what she did to Isla started to bubble as my words came hard and fast. "Sisters have one of the strongest bonds there is. She knew you longer than anyone else. You had a shared history, an innate understanding of each other's emotions. She should be your support system, loyal and honest. It's a lifelong friendship of shared values filled with empathy and unconditional love." I stopped, my breath unsteady. "At least, it's supposed to be."

Isla stared open-mouthed, her chest rising and falling at an alarming rate. Then suddenly, she rushed across the space between us and pulled me in close. Holding me tight, her tears were loud in my ear.

"I'm sorry you lost your sister, Aubrey. I'm sorry that was taken from you."

I allowed the hug, giving in to my own emotions, and for a short while, we stood holding each other, both lost in our grief.

I no longer believed Isla to be a killer.

CHAPTER ELEVEN

Once Isla composed herself, she made an excuse about checking catering and rushed from the room. I wasn't one hundred percent sure, but it felt like she'd been embarrassed by her outburst of affection. Maybe Chris hadn't been completely to blame with the marriage breakdown after all. But he had been guilty of the affair.

I still had a half hour before our last session of the weekend, and Daphne was starting to talk to me again. If I didn't get the words down now, I would forget them by the time that I made it home.

Sending a quick message to Spencer and Ellie that I was in the library, I opened my laptop and got to work.

Saltwater Bay had a permanent population of five thousand, but tourists would often triple that number during the height of summer. And winter. And every season in between. Tourism was the main source of income with the cave systems and white sandy beaches pulling people from near and far. The town was made up of an eclectic assortment of shops, and most of the locals were friendly. I say most as it would be a stretch to call Mr. Sandringham of Sandringham's Convenience Store friendly. On a happy day, cordial would be the best he ever got.

Driving down Main street, I slowed Bernie's Jeep Wrangler to a crawl, enjoying the breeze from the open windows. I waved to a few familiar faces and found a parking space outside Maeve's Mystic Moonstones. After grabbing my shoulder bag, I locked the car and took a moment to soak up the atmosphere. The day was already heating up with the humidity hitting the low nineties. And it was only nine a.m. Urgh.

Maeve's shop was tucked between The Salty Bean café and The Tattered Page bookstore. Her window was filled to the brim with crystals of all colors and varieties. I knew every morning Maeve perused the store saying good morning to the gems. Apparently, it set them up well for the day ahead, increasing the power of their energy. To be honest, I didn't know much about crystals, but whenever Bernie and I had visited Maeve in the store, I was always drawn to them. In particular, the beautiful blue and white pattern of the Larimar that reminded me of the ocean. The year Bernie had given me a bracelet made of it, I'd slipped it on my wrist and never taken it off. Like my grandmother, I too felt a kinship with the water.

Now as the bell jingled above the door when I pushed it open, my fingers fiddled with the smooth round beads, and its presence had a calming effect on me.

"Is that you Daphne?" Maeve's smile beamed at me from behind the counter.

My smile matched hers as I crossed the floor, passing row after row of crystal beads, suncatchers, and gorgeous jewelry. Wind chimes sang the song of the breeze, and the wooden boards beneath my feet gave the occasional creak.

Maeve's fluffy white cat Astro jumped from the shelf as she stepped around the counter, her arms wide, rushing toward me in a cloud of patchouli. Her long red and orange cotton top covered her bright blue tights, her shoulder length gray hair was highlighted with matching blue streaks, and her oversized silver earrings tinkled as she moved.

"How are you my dear?" Astro trotted toward the front window as Maeve engulfed me in a hug, and I had to fight back emotion. All my memories of Maeve and Astro were tied to Bernie, and a lump formed in my throat as tears stung my eyes.

Once she released me, I blinked hard and swallowed everything down. Bernie would hate for me to be sad, but seriously, how could I not be?

"It's been a stressful day." I sighed.

"Well, you look beautiful as always."

I caught sight of myself in the mirror behind the jewelry counter and thought Maeve was definitely losing her mind. My hair that I'd neatly tied in a band at my neck was now puffing out at odd angles, my mascara had smudged beneath my brown eyes, *and perspiration sat in awkward little clumps around my hairline. So, paradise had a few flaws, but I may as well get used to it as this was going to be my new normal.*

"Maeve, how do you look so together when the humidity is so high?"

She chuckled. "Hairspray. Lots of it. I may be slowly killing the ozone layer, but at least my hair doesn't frizz."

I attempted to smooth my locks as Maeve led the way to the counter.

"How are you settling in?" she asked, moving a large amethyst butterfly aside.

I sighed. "Have you heard about the skull found under my house?"

News travels fast in small towns, so I wasn't surprised when she nodded. "I heard it's Jenkins Butler." *The spark in her green eyes dimmed.*

"That's what the detective thought."

"Not a great start to your new life, is it, my dear?" *Maeve looked thoughtful for a second before moving toward a display of sage. Turning to me, she handed me the largest bunch she had.*

"Take this," *she said.* "You need to remove any negative spirits from the property. When you get back to the beach shack, light it until it smokes. Then walk around every room chanting this—I call upon the light to cleanse this space tonight. Negative spirits you must depart, leave this place, and heal my heart. Only love and light to remain, peace and harmony I reclaim."

As if I was going to remember that. Well, I guess I got the gist of it.

"Thanks, Maeve." *Admittedly, the earthy aroma of the sage and the lavender flowers that adorned it seemed to calm me already. Or maybe that was just being surrounded by so many crystals. I could definitely see why Maeve was always so chilled.*

"I've been worried about you, Daphne. Giving up your life to move here is a big leap."

"I love Saltwater Bay. And already I feel closer to Bernie. As soon as I walked into the beach shack, I felt like she was there with me."

"If I know Bernie like I think I do, she'll be following you around like a shadow. Even in death, she won't sit still." *Nostalgia twisted her smile.*

"I like that idea." My fingers found the smooth beads on my bracelet, and my heart warmed.

"I've got something for you. Give me a minute and I'll go and find it." Maeve disappeared behind a curtain that led to what I knew was a small kitchen and storeroom in the back of the shop.

Within seconds, I heard a lot of clattering and boxes being shuffled across the floor, Maeve huffing and Astro meowing. As she came back toward me, her hair was now slightly ruffled, and she had blood dripping down her arm.

"Maeve! You hurt yourself!"

"No, that was Astro. In his old age, he doesn't like to be disturbed when he's hiding amongst the stock." She shrugged and handed me a small, applique bag with long tassels, before pulling a handful of tissues from a nearby box.

"What's in this?" I asked, surprised.

"It's Bernie's bag. She carried it everywhere she went. The day of her accident, she'd visited me in the morning for our usual run down of events, but she must have forgotten to take it when she left. I was going to drop it to her later that day, but then..." Maeve's eyes filled with tears. Sniffing them away, she continued on, "Well, I forgot all about it after that. When I heard you were moving to town, I thought I'd keep hold of it for you."

"Have you looked inside?" I knew I would have.

"No. It's too... personal. Whenever I see it, I can't stop thinking about how I should have taken it to her earlier in the day. If I'd been there, maybe... maybe she'd still be alive."

"Oh, Maeve. You can't think like that. Bernie always told me that when your time is up, then it's up. There's nothing you can do to stop it."

Maeve took my hand and squeezed it. "You're so much like her, Daphne. She was so proud of the woman you've grown into."

It was my turn for the tears to well up. "If I can be half the woman she was, then I'll be happy."

Maeve handed me the tissue box as we took a moment, lost in our own thoughts about Bernie. Once we'd both composed ourselves, she straightened her top, swiped at some stray mascara under her eyes, and smiled.

"Now, what are you going to do for work? I can offer you some hours in the shop."

I sniffed. "That's a really lovely offer, but thankfully, being a virtual assistant to one of the country's up-and-coming influencers means I can work from anywhere."

"What exactly does a virtual assistant do? Is it like a secretary?"

"Pretty much. Only I don't have to sit in a stuffy office. Instead, I get to enjoy all of this." I swung my arms around me and bumped the large amethyst butterfly. I cringed.

Maeve shook her head smiling as she effortlessly adjusted it. "It astounds me how the world works these days."

"The joys of the internet." I shrugged before securely tucking my hands under my arms.

"Well, if any of that changes, my offer stands. I would love to have you around here more often." Maeve beamed, and I felt Bernie hug my shoulders.

I hadn't set out to write Emily as my main character. But now looking back over Daphne, I could see her in every tiny detail. And I knew it was because a part of me was letting go of the grief I felt for her. I was allowing life to once again permeate my mind and excitement to fill my soul. I'd clamped that down over the last year, afraid to do her an injustice by being happy. But that's what she would have wanted for me. Above all else, I knew Emily only ever wanted what was right for me. Having her live on through Daphne meant I could spend time with her whenever I wanted to, sending her on adventures she never got to have, and falling in love with the man of her dreams.

I swiped a silent tear and quickly checked the time before I dropped everything into my tote and rushed upstairs to throw the last of my things in my suitcase. Luckily, I'd packed most of it before breakfast, but I wanted to check under the bed for anything I may have dropped and to ensure all chargers were safely locked away in my bag.

I had a very bad habit of losing chargers, and these days, money was tighter than I would have liked. And if I wanted to keep doing things like retreats, then I needed to monitor my spending on unnecessary items.

The card I'd had everyone sign for Isla poked out from the top of my bag, and I took a moment to open it and read the messages we'd all written, thanking her for the weekend and giving her our support and love. There were only six of us here, but as expected when given the opportunity to write, an author would do exactly that.

I smiled at the mini novels each of us had written, but my gaze stopped on the flowery writing that belonged to Nancy. She had a very distinctive flourish, and I was mesmerized by the beauty of it compared to my scrawl.

But hang on, why did her writing look so familiar? I'd seen it before. Only where? It had to have been over the weekend as we'd barely known each other before that.

Closing my eyes, I slowed my breathing and thought it through. Something in my subconscious was niggling at me, and I needed to give it the space to be heard.

"What are you trying to tell me?" I asked. It was a strange technique, but one that worked on more than one occasion. "Where have I seen that writing before, and why is it important?"

Recent memories swirled through my mind, the colors mixing as images fell into place. And that's when it hit me. The letter *P* was very recognizable.

Snapping my eyes open, I grabbed my phone, my heart beating at an erratic rate. Hitting dial, I sat up straight, willing the line to hurry up and connect.

"Aubrey?" Tate's strong voice reverberated in my ear, filling me with warmth and safety.

"I think I know who wrote the note. And I think she killed Willow."

I just didn't know why.

* * *

I'd learned my lesson. There was no way I was going to question Nancy. Nope, I'd do exactly what Tate had asked and stay put until he got here.

My heart was beating quickly as adrenalin flooded my body, but I used the energy to pack the last of my belongings away. Dragging my case into the hallway, I wanted to find Spencer and Ellie and tell them what I'd learned.

The wheels of my case trundled against the floorboards as I made my way toward the stairs.

Ellie's room was right next door to Nancy's, but I kept my focus on what I was doing and knocked on Ellie's door.

Ellie screamed, only it didn't come from within her room. It came from Nancy's.

Without thinking twice, I charged Nancy's door. As I did, a loud shot rang out, followed by another scream.

"Ellie!" Her name flew from my lips as I barged my way in. I had no idea what I was going to find, but I didn't care. My friend was in a murderer's room, and she needed my help. "Ellie!"

As the door flung back, bouncing off the wall and ricocheting behind me, Ellie stood on the opposite side of the room with her eyes wide and her face pale. Thankfully, she was uninjured. I planned to keep it that way.

"Oh, my goodness," Nancy cried. "That was loud! Ahhhhh! Aubrey. You scared me."

I'd scared her? "Nancy! What are you doing?"

The beam of sunlight from the window glittered against the shiny barrel of Nancy's revolver that she held near her head, and a trickle of blood dripped from her earlobe.

"I'm sorry," Nancy stated, her shoulders squared, her back straight as she lowered the gun and clasped her ear. "I missed. I've never used a gun before, and I missed. Geez, that ringing is loud!"

"Nancy, what are you doing? Please put down the gun. Ellie hasn't done anything to hurt you. Please don't shoot her." A wave of nausea hit me hard as thoughts that I could lose Ellie, too, caused my legs to shake and weakness to consume me.

Our gaze locked as Ellie slowly shook her head, her feet seemingly glued to the floor.

"I'm not going to hurt Ellie." Fatigue sat heavy in Nancy's eyes as she pushed her glasses up the bridge of her nose. "No. No. You have it all wrong. Ellie's just in the wrong place at the wrong time. I tried to explain that to her, but she wouldn't leave."

I reached for the wall for support as my gaze shot around the room. The bed was neatly made, everything was clean and tidy, and her suitcase zipped. But the note on the bedside table, held in place by a half-torn notebook, caused me to pause.

As the pieces fell into place in my mind, Nancy stood perfectly still, the gun now pushed hard against her temple, her skin deathly pale, her lips pulled tight as tears pooled behind her lashes.

"I'm sorry. I did request that, if Ellie wouldn't leave, then she was to stay on that side of the room and close her eyes. This is a very weird angle to hold a gun and pull the trigger. I'm worried I might not do a neat job of it."

"Put the gun down," I commanded, my hands shaking as I lifted my palms toward her and wished I hadn't opened the door.

"Aubrey, you need to get out of here. Take her with you," Nancy pleaded. "You both seem like lovely women. I do not want you haunted by my death."

"Exactly! You don't want us to have to live with that, do you?" Even though at the rate my heart was palpitating, I may not live that long. "Why don't you put the gun down, and we'll chat about what's going on?"

"It's not that simple!"

I jumped at her sudden outburst and pulled back, my butt hitting the door and accidentally pushing it shut. Oh geez. Now I'd closed both Ellie and myself in a room with a killer. *What the heck is wrong with you, Aubrey?*

"I'm sure you're exaggerating the problem," I trilled, going for upbeat in the hope I could persuade her I was right, and maybe—just maybe—she would put the gun down and not kill any of us. "After all, we authors have great imaginations." I looked at Ellie, hoping to get her attention and her help, only she seemed too shocked to move.

"No. No," Nancy continued, waving the gun around frantically. "There is no imagination involved. I have to live with what I did, and I can't do that. I've tried to tell myself it was an accident—which it was—but I killed Willow. I killed her, Aubrey!"

Tears burst the dam that had been holding them back, and they tumbled over the deep wrinkles in her tortured face.

"I know. But from what I've learned there's a long list of people who had a good reason to kill her! She had an affair and fell pregnant possibly by her brother-in-law, used her latest boyfriend in order to get a publishing deal with the biggest publishers in the country, and stole money from her business partner." I ticked my fingers as I spoke. "A number of people wanted her dead. Turns out she wasn't a very nice person."

Nancy blinked rapidly as her jaw slackened, and she momentarily struggled to get her words together.

"W-well… well, I never knew that." Nancy stared out the window for a moment, and I took the chance to signal Ellie.

My eyes were wide as I nodded toward the gun and then the door, silently telling her to sneak out while she could. Only her eyes were locked on Nancy as she paled and clung to the wall.

Dizziness swirled my vision, and I felt lightheaded, but I took a slow breath and tried to stop the worst-case scenario playing like a movie in my head. None of that was going to help Ellie, and as Nancy waved the gun in the air, I pushed back against the adrenaline surge and tried to still my mind.

Nancy's words came slow and controlled. "Despite what she did to those people, Aubrey, they didn't push her out the window, did they?" Her hand shook as she lifted the gun to her temple, and I closed my eyes thinking she was about to pull the trigger.

Banging on the door behind me caused me to scream and stars to appear in my eyes. The dizziness threatened to take me down as a cold sweat broke out on my forehead, and the urge to turn and run was overwhelming. But that wasn't the answer. Ellie needed my help, and despite knowing that Nancy had killed Willow, and she needed to pay for what she had done, this wasn't the right way to go about it.

"Go away!" Nancy yelled. "Please!"

"Nancy! What's going on?" Chris's voice was loud through the wooden door.

She looked at me, her eyes wide. "This wasn't supposed to be like this," she hissed, hysteria playing in her tone. "You all need to go away and leave me alone. I'm sure I'll get it right this time."

"Ellie, you go and tell Chris that Nancy is a bit upset. Ellie!" Her head spun toward me, and she blinked, seemingly coming to.

"Wh-what?" she whispered.

"Ellie, please go. Get out of this room."

"Come with me," Ellie urged.

"No. I can't leave Nancy to do this." I held Ellie's gaze, silently pleading that she get some help. She nodded her understanding.

"Nancy?" Chris's voice echoed toward us, making me jump. "What's going on?"

"Nancy, Chris is going to want an explanation as to why you blew a hole in his painting." I wanted to distract her as Ellie tiptoed past me.

"I'm sorry, Chris," she yelled. "Please pay for all damages with the credit card you have of mine on file!"

I knew Tate was on his way. I just wished he would hurry the heck up.

The door behind me pushed open, but as Nancy squeezed her eyes shut, her hand holding the gun wobbling around, I pushed back against it. Ellie froze.

"It's okay, Chris," I called. "Ellie and I are here with Nancy. We're just going to have a chat. Maybe you could go downstairs and wait for any visitors who may be arriving?" I hoped he got the hint as to what was going on, but I wasn't sure I was that clear. Thankfully, he did stop trying to get into the room as hushed voices sounded outside.

"Why don't you tell me what happened? Explain it all," I said, trying to keep my voice calm. "Start at the beginning."

Ellie slowly took her phone from her pocket and typed a message while I distracted Nancy.

"It's all in the letter I wrote." She gestured to the bedside table

"Sure, but I'd rather hear it from you."

"Don't try to talk me out of this, Aubrey."

"I won't. But author to author, tell me your story. One last time."

She looked hesitant, but after some internal debate, she appeased me. "Fine, but I'm not putting the gun down. You might try to take it from me."

That thought wasn't one that I was processing. In fact, I wanted to be as far from it as I could get.

"I promise I'll stay right here."

"And you'll keep your hands where I can see them?"

"Uh-huh. Scouts honor." I dropped my hands to my side and tried my best to look relaxed.

"Okay then. Well…" She took a moment, lost to her thoughts, but when her eyes connected with mine, she started to talk. "The book that Willow had written, the one she got the Heron and Heron publishing deal for, wasn't hers. She stole it from me."

I jolted, shocked by her revelation. "Okay."

"A few years ago, my husband Robert got very sick. We didn't have a lot of time, and what we did have we spent in the hospital. Do you know how long the days are when you're sitting around a hospital?"

I didn't, but I nodded my encouragement.

"Robert would kill time by telling me stories that he made up, and they would always make me laugh or keep me on the edge of my seat. His favorites were the thrillers." She stopped for a breath, her eyes lost to the memories as a smile whispered across her lips. "I decided one day to take a notebook. He could dictate the story, and I would write his words. It was nothing serious, but it kept our minds busy. In the beginning, the story was something fun for us to write. But I quickly realized we had something special there. A unique novel filled with romance and suspense. Turns out, Robert was quite the author."

Her chin lifted as her eyes gleamed. "Every day, I would visit him in the hospital and hand write the words he spoke into my notebook." Her gaze flicked to the torn book on the bedside table. "Oh, the twists and turns that he came up with were amazing! By the end of the day, my hand ached from trying to keep up with the speed he retold his tale, but I couldn't wait to find out what he was going to say next." Her laugh was faint as she took a moment before continuing, "Only as the weeks went on, his voice got weaker, and the story telling slowed. Until one day the tales stopped, and I had to say goodbye to my best friend."

Her laughter was replaced with tears as they spilled over the edge of her lashes, and I gave her a moment in her grief. "The hospital gave me his belongings, and I put them away with the book. My world was destroyed, and I was unsure as to whether I would ever be able to get myself up again."

Tears ran down my own cheeks as I felt the pain in her words. I understood that feeling of not being able to get up, not wanting to talk to anyone, to lock the world out because you couldn't deal with any of it. And the only people who truly knew why you were acting the way you were, were those that had experienced it themselves.

"Do you believe in ghosts, Aubrey? Do you believe our deceased loved ones visit us in our dreams?"

I nodded.

"Well, I didn't. Until one night I dreamt that Robert was sitting on the bed alongside me, holding my hand, and telling me that he had written the final chapter to the story before he'd died.

Upon waking, I went in search of his belongings—the ones that the hospital had given me. I'd never had the strength to open that bag before, as I knew it was the last thing he'd worn, his slippers still molded to the shape of his feet. Immediately, I was surrounded by his scent, and in that moment, I felt him standing alongside me, willing me forward. But in that bag, there was also an envelope. A letter he had written telling me how the story ends." She swallowed hard.

"Only I didn't have the storytelling abilities necessary to pull it all together, so I set it all aside, unsure of what to do next. Then one day, I came across the opportunity to work with the famous Willow Fox. For an exorbitant fee, she promised to help me turn Robert's story into a real book. Can you imagine? Robert's name on the cover of a best seller?" Nancy's eyes filled with warmth. "Of course, I have no idea how to use a computer, so Willow asked me to give her the notebook, and she would have her assistant set it up in a Word file for me, and then Willow would work with me to improve it."

"Is that what you were working on this weekend?"

"No. Willow had advised me while she was getting everything set up that it would be a good idea to get one of Robert's other stories down before I forgot the details. So, I gave her the notebooks I'd used and decided to purchase a laptop. Robert had always been one to tell a tale, and if I could get them down before I forgot them, maybe he could have two books." She beamed.

"Why didn't you handwrite those too?"

"Well, Willow explained to me how important it was to have everything on a computer, and I couldn't afford to have her convert another story." Her shoulders drooped. "To be honest with you, the whole thing has made me grateful that I worked with plants my entire life. Staring at a screen all day and attempting to get the software to do what I want is a nightmare. It made me consider paying her to do the second book."

"I'm sure Robert would be very proud of you," I encouraged. Nancy had lowered the gun, so I was hopeful that my tactic was working.

"No. No he wouldn't. He'd be beyond disappointed at how naïve I am. I always have been. It's just that Willow was so nice, so trustworthy. Or so I thought. I learned the truth in our one-on-one session, when I asked her about the story, and she kept pushing it aside and brushing me off. I felt really uneasy about it all and asked for the notebooks back. She told me that Naomi was still working on it, but later when I asked Naomi, she said she didn't know anything about it." Nancy sat heavily in the chair by the window and looked down at the gun in her hands. "I wanted to ask Willow why she was lying, so when we had our break, I went to her room. And that's when I saw it. The typed manuscript of her latest novel—*The Black Rose*—right alongside the publishing contract with Heron and Heron. The tagline on the front summed up Robert's book perfectly. I picked it up, confused. But as I flipped the pages I recognized the words. She'd stolen his book. The book that was supposed to have Robert's name as the author now had giant letters stating Willow Fox! And do you know what she did? She smirked!"

Nancy stood, running her hands through her hair, the gun dangerously close to her skull.

"She denied it being Robert's, said I had no proof that it was. Well, the only proof I had were the notebooks where I had handwritten it all. And I'd stupidly given it to her. I trusted her! She had promised she would help me publish it for Robert. It was going to be his legacy. He would have been so proud. And she'd stolen that! But she denied all of it! And she gloated. There she was standing at the open window, laughing. But she underestimated me.

"I saw one of my notebooks sticking out from under a pile of manuscripts on her bed, and I grabbed it. It was my proof that the story was mine! Only Willow was quick, and she snatched at it, the pages ripping in her grip." Nancy rubbed her face, her tears intermingling with her fingers. Her voice thickened. "Before I knew what I was doing, I had my hands around her neck, and I pushed her as hard as I could. When she hit the window ledge, she lost her balance and fell. I didn't mean to kill her, Aubrey. I just wanted Robert's story back." Her chin lowered to her chest as she slowly shook her head.

Pieces of the puzzle started to click into place.

"It was you that hit me. You were in my room last night."

"Yes. When I saw you in the dining room last night with the detective, I overheard you all talking about the pages you found, and I knew it wouldn't take him long to piece it all together. If I could get it back from you, then I may be okay."

"Only you didn't realize I'd already given them to Detective Tate."

Nancy sighed heavily. "I'm not cut out for this."

"I know that feeling."

Nancy and I locked gazes, and an understanding passed between us.

"And after Willow… you know." I tumbled my hand over, indicating how she fell. "You made your escape down the secret stairs?"

Nancy nodded, and I knew I needed to keep her talking until I figured a way to get the gun out of her hands. "But how did you know about them?"

"I saw one of the cleaners use the door in the dining room and decided to check out where it led. I figured an old house like this would be riddled with secret passages." Her shoulders dropped as a long breath escaped her. "To think of the stories these walls could tell."

"Great place for a writing retreat," I agreed. "You must have been excited to have been offered a spot?" I inched closer, hoping she wouldn't notice. Ellie moved closer to the door, looking ready to run when I gave her the signal.

"I was. All of my dreams of honoring Robert's memory were coming together. I was starting work on his short stories, and I couldn't wait to see his novel resembling a real book." Nancy sank to the bed, her hands covering her eyes, the gun still clutched in her fingers. "But then it all went so horribly wrong. Oh my. How did I mess this all up so badly?"

"It's okay. You have the proof now that Robert wrote the book. You can contact Heron and Heron, and I'm sure they will still publish it with his name on it." I was sure it wasn't as easy as that, but now wasn't the time to point that out.

"That's true." Her head shot up, her red-rimmed eyes wide. "Now, where is it?" Nancy pushed up off the bed, only footsteps pounding outside of her room pulled her up short.

"Nancy!" Loud knocks pummeled the door. "It's Detective Tate."

Nancy froze, Ellie squealed, and I may or may not have peed my pants.

"What's he doing here?" Nancy asked.

Oh geez. Now didn't feel like a good time to tell her that I'd called him.

"Maybe you can tell him what you told me. Explain the whole situation. I'm sure he'll understand," I suggested.

"Aubrey. You can't be serious? The man will send me directly to jail! I can't go to jail. Do you know what the ladies at tennis will say? How I've tarnished Robert's memory?" Her hand once again shook as she moved the gun to her temple. "No. No. I can't live with that. This way is far better. I know Robert is waiting for me on the other side. We'll be together once again."

"Wait! Please, hear me out. If you pull that trigger, then his book will be published under Willow's name, and no one will ever know the truth."

"You can tell them."

"Me? No!" I was about to go into the reasons why I wasn't the right person for that job, when the door behind me burst open, pushing me into Nancy. Ellie fell to the floor as Detective Tate rushed into the room, two uniformed officers flanked behind him.

I jumped as my heart rate moved into the danger zone, and Nancy squealed, grabbing my arm and pulling me in close.

As the cold hard nozzle of her gun was pushed into my neck, I knew things had gone downhill very quickly.

"Take it easy, Nancy." Tate spoke slowly, his hands raised, showing us both he had no weapon. "We're only here to talk to you. Why don't you let Aubrey go, and we can sit down and have a chat?"

"I can't do that." Nancy's voice trembled.

"Why not?" Tate asked calmly.

"I'm no expert on negotiations, but the two uniformed officers with their guns pointed at me tells me you might not be in a talking mood."

She had a point.

Tate looked over his shoulder. "Lower your weapons," he commanded.

Both officers looked unsure but followed orders.

As steel dug harder into my flesh, I whimpered, doing my best to slow my breathing and control my blood pressure. Otherwise, I was going to die of a stroke long before Nancy could shoot me.

"See?" Tate turned back to Nancy. "I just want to talk."

I felt Nancy relax, and as Tate gave her a friendly smile, she faltered.

It was all I needed.

I lifted my hand up to her arm and pushed the gun forward and away, simultaneously grabbing her wrist. She was a lightweight and had not anticipated my move. The gun fell from her grip, and I tightened my hold on her arm and waited for Tate to take control.

He was fast, and within seconds, he had her in handcuffs. He then passed her to the uniformed officers who read her Miranda rights.

Nancy looked more than dazed, and for a moment, I thought she might pass out. But then Tate stepped toward me, his body blocking her from my view, and my heart beat an erratic tune for a completely different reason.

"How do you know moves like that?" he asked, looking suitably impressed.

I shrugged. "Community self-defense class."

Tate nodded appreciatively.

"It helped that Nancy didn't see it coming. I'm sure if I used the move on you, I wouldn't have been as successful."

"Maybe one day we'll give that a go and find out."

As the uniformed officers opened the door to lead Nancy away, I saw the crowd gathered outside the door.

Spencer had his arm around Ellie almost holding her up. Her face was deathly white, she was shaking uncontrollably, and she blinked at an alarming rate. Spencer looked like every muscle in his body had tensed. His lips were a tight line, and his breathing was fast. Both of my friends had been scared senseless. Again.

I figured it was time to only write about crime. My days as a real-life investigator were over.

* * *

Ellie, Spencer, and I were standing in the open entryway, our suitcases packed and ready to head home. A surreal calm had descended on the Grand Hotel once Nancy had been taken away in a patrol vehicle. Word had spread very quickly amongst the guests as to what had really happened, and despite everyone knowing the truth, there was an unspoken sympathy for what Willow had done to Nancy.

"Well, that was an exciting end to an exciting weekend." Beverley's cheeks glowed as she and Kara moved in behind us. "If all retreats are like this one, I think I might make a habit of attending them."

Kara cocked a hip and pursed her lips. "Maybe, but the next one should be genre based. Specifically for erotic romance writers. What do you think, Aubrey? Want me to let you know if I find one?"

Heat flushed my face. "Umm, I'm good thank you. But thanks for thinking of me."

She shrugged. "Your loss. Anyone else?" Her open gaze traveled over the three of us. "What about you, Spence? You could learn a trick or two."

"I'll pass. But if I ever write a thriller that needs some spice, you'll be the first person I call for advice."

Kara's face lit up like a Christmas tree.

"Are you ladies heading home?" Ellie asked.

"Yeah. I think the snow's coming early, and if I don't head off now, I might not beat it," Beverley explained. "I'm dropping Kara off in Snohomish on my way past."

"My man's driving up to meet me for a mini vacation." Kara bounced on her toes before pushing past us and heading to the parking lot. "Come on, Bev. Stop wasting time. I've got things to do." Her eyebrows jiggled. "It was nice meeting you all. Maybe we'll bump into each other at a future event."

Beverley gave a small wistful sigh. "Oh, to be her age again and have her libido."

I was her age, and I didn't have anywhere near that kind of libido.

As we waved them goodbye, Jenna hurried over to us, her brow low and her shoulders tense.

"You okay?" Ellie asked her.

"No! I can't believe that Willow was stealing other people's work and labelling it as her own! And I helped her rework a section of it, thinking how amazingly clever she was!" Jenna fists balled into her eye sockets, anger simmering in her every move.

"Don't beat yourself up, Jenna," Ellie cooed. "How were you to know what Willow had been up to?"

"You figured it out!"

"No, I didn't," Ellie responded. "Despite the lists of suspects and motives that I'd written, I had no idea what had really happened."

"Then why did you confront Nancy?" Spencer asked.

"I didn't. I stumbled across her holding a gun on herself by accident. Do you know how many times this weekend I've mixed her door up for mine? It was Aubrey who solved it."

A small glow of pride blossomed behind my breastbone, but as Jenna's shoulders slumped and tears gathered behind her lashes, I swallowed it down hard.

As she looked at me, she said, "Do you think the real reason Willow agreed to do the retreats was with the intention of stealing manuscripts from unsuspecting new authors? Or is that terrible of me to think that way?"

Ellie grabbed her arm and held tight. "You're not responsible for any of this. Whatever her motives were had nothing to do with you."

"But how could she have implicated me in something so awful?" she whispered.

"Greed. It's the root of all evil." Ellie pulled Jenna in close and gave her a hug.

"I thought money was the root of all evil," I added.

"Same thing," Spencer said. "Only I think Willow may have wanted more than money. I think the fame was a big motive for her too."

"Yeah, from what we've learned, Willow wanted it all. The fame, the money, and the attention. Unfortunately, Nancy put her trust in the wrong person." Ellie released Jenna and looked across the lawn. I followed her gaze, stopping on Isla as she turned her back on Chris and stomped away.

"She wasn't the only one," I commented, wondering how a woman ever got over that kind of betrayal.

"Did we ever find out who the real father of Willow's baby was?" Ellie asked.

"Berkley told me it was his," Spencer announced.

I spun toward him, shocked. "You saw Berkley?"

"Yeah. He was in the men's bathroom. He looked visibly upset, and I gave him a sympathetic ear. Turns out despite Willow only using him to get a contract with Heron and Heron, he really did have feelings for her and had been looking forward to becoming a father."

"Wow." Jenna released a slow whistle. "What's he like? Is he as enigmatic as he looks?"

"Well, the urinal does take some of the mystique away from a person." Spencer shrugged.

"But you spoke to him. In real life." Ellie's eyes were wide as she was seduced by the infamous Jonathan Berkley. Admittedly, I too was quite impressed Spencer had been so close to the legend.

"Yeah, but only for a short while. It's not like we're best buddies. He was there. He looked upset, and I felt bad for the guy. It didn't take much for him to spill his feelings."

"Why has he been hiding from us all?" I know if I was as famous as he was, I'd happily show my face to my adoring readers.

Spencer shrugged. "Said he wanted to lie low for a while. Didn't want people to know he was here. Then after Willow died, he got very drunk and hid out in his room for a few days. And before you ask me anything else, that's all I know as he quickly shut up when Levi came in. There's a bit of tension between those two."

"Geez, it's all happening in the men's bathroom!"

Ellie threw me a look that told me to shush up because she wanted the gossip. "What did Levi do?" she asked.

"Saw Berkley and threatened to kill him. My suggestion was that wasn't a great idea after what had happened to Nancy, and he left in a huff. Last I saw him, he was spinning tires in his hurry to drive away from here."

"You know the bit I don't understand?" I mused. "How did all these men love Willow as much as they did?"

"Narcissists have a way of making those around them fall in love before they realize what they're getting into." Spencer looked down at his hands as he spoke, and I wondered if he'd experienced it.

I'd never been in love, so I couldn't comment.

Tate meandered across the gravel driveway toward the entryway and stopped in front of me, smiling. Not a great earth-shattering smile, but one that shone directly into my soul and made my heart stutter a tiny little bit.

"Aubrey, when you get a chance, can you stop by the station?" he asked. "I'll need you to make an official statement."

I nodded. "What'll happen to Nancy?"

"She'll be processed and then will get a bail hearing. After that, the system decides her fate. But we're also investigating the theft of her work. Once we prove that, it could throw some sympathy her way and a jury may proceed lightly."

"And the world will know that the great Willow Fox wasn't as great as everyone thought she was," Ellie added.

"No, she wasn't. But preliminary checks prove she didn't steal the book alone. She had an accomplice."

"Oh! Who?" I asked, curiosity prickling my scalp.

"I'm not at liberty to say at this point." Tate glanced across the driveway, his gaze stopping on Chris. My thoughts jumped to the email Willow had sent him about the manuscript being their little secret. "But once I've gathered the evidence, an arrest will be made."

"I spoke to Isla before she left." Jenna cut in to my thoughts. "Apparently, she's the sole heir to Willow's estate. Once it's all settled, she told me that she's going to speak to Heron and Heron and see if they will still publish the book listing Nancy's husband as the author. I know what Nancy did was wrong, but it will be nice she'll get the resolution they deserved."

"That's lovely," Ellie agreed.

"As we all know it's extremely difficult to get a publishing deal with Heron and Heron, and even though Willow's name won't be propelling the sales of the book, I'd imagine it will still do well," Jenna added. "It should give Nancy the money she's going to need for legal bills."

Spencer grunted. "I get it. The theft of your work is terrible, and the circumstances around it just add to that, but let's not forget she's a murderer."

"Actually, the charges are manslaughter," Tate corrected him. "Nancy didn't know her work had been stolen until she was in the room with Willow, which means she didn't go to the meeting with the intent to kill her."

"Yes, but when Nancy realized what Willow had done, she should have gone to the police about it. Willow would still be alive and would be the one facing charges." Spencer's eyes narrowed and his back stiffened.

Tate threw his hands up in surrender. "I'm not arguing with you on that point. But hindsight is a wonderful thing. We're all a lot clearer and more reasonable when we're not emotionally involved."

My thoughts darted back to what Spencer had told me about Tate and why he'd relocated to Snohomish. Is that how he felt about what he'd done? Had he acted from an emotional place?

"What will happen to Ricky?" Spencer asked. "Will he be arrested for blackmailing Chris?"

Tate shook his head. "At this stage, Chris hasn't pressed charges, but that could change. Either way, I'll look into it."

I released a long slow breath. "Investigating is hard."

"Does that mean you're going to stick to only writing about it from now on?" Tate turned those gray eyes on me, pinning me to the spot.

"Heck yeah. In fact, I might change genres and write romance from now on. Surely, that will be a lot less dangerous."

"Not for the heart it won't," Ellie added.

Urgh! Maybe it was time to work in my mom's bakery after all.

EPILOGUE

"Maeve, did you know if Bernie and Jenkins Butler were a couple?"

A bevy of wrinkles appeared on her forehead. "Briefly. They went out to dinner a few times, he showed her around the caves, and she was teaching him to surf. Didn't last very long though, as he went missing around then."

"How was Bernie?"

"About him missing? Well, she was upset. She always had a big heart, and I think even though their friendship was brief, she felt a kinship with him. Why do you ask?"

"The detective was asking me about it. I was surprised as she never mentioned him to me."

"She kept her romantic interests quiet from her family. Your mom never liked the idea of her being with men other than your pop."

That sounded like Mom. "She worried about Bernie all the time. Was worried a man would take advantage of a woman so open to helping everyone."

Maeve shook her head. "Bernie was sharp. She could spot a conman a mile away."

"So, Butler was a good guy?"

"I didn't know him, to be honest." Maeve picked up the amethyst butterfly and placed it on the shelf behind her.

"But you know everyone in this town."

"Well, yes. I knew him. I just didn't know much about him. He came over from the mainland when our mayor, Robert Bunt, decided to open the caves to the public. Butler advised him on safety and what not and then stayed on for a few years as caretaker."

"Didn't the caves belong to the indigenous?"

"Uh-uh, but they worked together with Butler, and everyone benefited."

"Did he ever have any disagreements with them? Was anyone ever unhappy with the way he did things?"

"He ruffled the odd feather or two, but people in this town generally get along. There's something very calming about Saltwater Bay. It's a special place that brings out the best in people."

Yeah, I felt that every time I visited, which was why I jumped at the chance to uproot my life and move into the beach shack.

"Why are you asking?" Maeve cocked an eyebrow.

"Just curious about the man whose remains washed up under my house." I shrugged. "The police believe he was murdered, and even though I'm not a massive believer in the divine, I do believe everything happens for a reason. What that reason is I'm yet to learn."

I sat back in my chair and smiled. *Murder for Shore* was taking shape. I knew exactly who murdered Jenkins Butler, and I couldn't wait to lay it all out on the page. Stretching my fingers, I readied myself for the next chapter, but the doorbell shook me from my imaginary world and back to reality.

Wondering who it could be, I pushed backwards from my desk and moved the twelve steps to the door.

The wind had picked up over the last few days and was rocking my home despite the fact I'd tied it as tightly to the mooring as I could. Snow had fallen just as Beverley had predicted it would. I already had my bubblers in place in the water, ready to keep the ice at bay, the firewood was chopped, and my fire was roaring. My little home was as prepared as I could make it, ready for the freezing winter months.

My parents hated my houseboat, wanting me to live somewhere much more secure, but I loved it. I loved that it was tiny because it felt cozy. I loved the water view that I had from the floor to ceiling windows from the lounge room, and I loved the family of ducks that visited every morning waiting for the hugely expensive duck food that I'd purchased just for them.

Reaching the front door, I pushed the blind aside to see who my visitor was. I swallowed hard as Detective Tate shuffled from one foot to the other, his jaw flexed. I hurriedly checked my reflection in the mirror, fluffed my hair, smoothed my shirt, and swiped at the stray mascara dot under my eye. Satisfied this was as good as it was going to get in the next few seconds, I smiled and opened the door.

"Good morning," I cooed, willing my heartbeat to settle into its normal rhythm. It had been a couple of weeks since the incident at the Grand Hotel, and I'd barely heard from Tate since. Spencer, on the other hand, had decided to stay in Stoney Creek for a while longer to work on his manuscript and had been making daily stops to chat about writing and our craft. Despite Ellie's protests that this was just an excuse, I didn't push anything romantic. If Spencer had an interest, he would show his hand when he was ready.

"Aubrey." Tate's smile was tight. "Would you mind if I came in?" His tone was gentle, yet his shoulders were tense, and my stomach clenched. An air of foreboding followed him as I stepped aside.

"Of course. I can make a fresh pot of coffee if you'd like one."

He waited for me to lead the way through to the kitchen. My home wasn't big, so it didn't take long.

"No. Thanks though but this isn't a social visit." He glanced around, and I could see him taking in every detail.

My stomach did a full flip as my throat thickened.

"What's wrong?" I asked, reaching the kitchen and grabbing the countertop for support. "You're a long way from home. Is it Ellie? Or Spencer? Are they hurt?"

He shook his head. "No. No. It's nothing like that. Why don't you take a seat, and we can talk."

"Please. Just tell me what's wrong."

His Adam's apple bobbed, and thoughts flicked through his eyes as they held mine. I knew he was considering his words carefully.

"Okay, well. Do you remember when you told me about your sister and the accident she was in?"

I nodded, confusion pushing some anxiety aside.

"Your words made me look into it further."

My thoughts froze momentarily as I bit my lip. I knew he'd been looking into it long before I said those words.

"Do you mind if we sit?" he asked, rubbing the back of his neck as he gazed around my home. "In fact, can we sit outside in the fresh air?"

"Sure. It's cold though."

"That's okay. The cold air helps me think."

I reluctantly let go of the counter and led the way to the small deck off the front of the house. The freezing water gently lapped the sides of my houseboat, and the frosty air bit into my skin as I sat opposite Tate. Only I barely felt any of it, waiting for him to move the conversation back to my sister's accident.

"Tate, what's going on?"

Rubbing his hands together, he leaned his elbows on his knees before lifting his eyes to meet mine. "Aubrey, when I learned what happened to Emily, an alarm bell rang in my mind. It was loud enough that I decided to look into the reports taken on the day of the accident."

"And?"

"And I don't think it actually was an accident."

My own alarm bells started to ring in my ears as I considered what he'd said. "How could it not be? She fell asleep behind the wheel, ran off the road, and hit a tree. She died instantly." Admittedly, there were no witnesses to corroborate that.

"Yes, I know. But there was something about it that sounded familiar to me. It reminded me of a case that I was a part of in New York. The scene was so similar. A young woman in her late-twenties who had spent the evening with friends at the local bar. Her friends reported a man with a spider tattoo on his arm buying her a drink. The woman turned him down only to later die in an unexplained road accident."

"So what really happened to her?"

"The man that she turned down followed her and ran her off the road."

Nausea swirled at the thought. "Did you catch him?"

"No. We found a witness who saw the car following her, but it was a stolen vehicle, and we could never find the man responsible."

"What does this have to do with Emily?"

"The night she died, Emily's friends reported she'd turned down the offer of a drink from a stranger. She declined his advances and not long after left to head home alone. On the way, for no apparent reason, her car left the road at an uncharacteristic speed, killing her instantly."

Hearing the details of that night once again caused the bile to rise in my throat as memories of Mom calling me with the news sat heavy in my mind.

"I'm so sorry, Aubrey." Tate gently took my hand in his, his touch soothing and supportive. "The detective who got Emily's case quickly wrote it off as an accident, but checking his notes, in my honest opinion, he didn't do his job properly. I followed up on a few of his leads and found the footage of the night she was at the bar. I recognized the man who purchased that drink for her. It was the same guy who purchased the drink for the woman in New York."

"What exactly are you saying?"

"I'm saying I think these cases are connected. I'm positive that Emily was murdered."

WHAT TO READ THE REST OF AUBREY JACKSON'S *MURDER FOR* SHORE NOVELLA?

Get your copy from Gemma Halliday Publishing now, wherever ebooks are sold!

ABOUT THE AUTHOR

USA Today bestselling author Beth Prentice lives on the gorgeous Sunshine Coast in Queensland. She writes funny, romantic mysteries (aka cozy mysteries), paranormal cozy mysteries, and the odd rom com because two of her favorite things are romance and mystery.

When she's not writing you can find her lost in a good book, passively watching documentaries, or scrolling Instagram and dreaming of perfect hair. She loves a good chat so feel free to reach out to her anytime!

To learn more about Beth Prentice, visit her online at:
https://bethprenticenovels.com

To see more of Beth Prentice's books from Gemma Halliday Publishing, including the Murder By the Book Mysteries, her Saltwater Bay Secrets Mysteries co-authored with Aubrey Jackson, and her contributions to the Aloha Lagoon Mysteries, visit us online at:
www.gemmahallidaypublishing.com/beth-prentice

Printed in Dunstable, United Kingdom